DELLA MORTIKA
THE CIRCUS OF SECRETS

GERALDINE F. MARTIN

ILLUSTRATIONS BY
PAUL J. MARTIN & MARISA MARTIN

VIVID
PUBLISHING

Published by Vivid Publishing
P.O. Box 948, Fremantle
Western Australia 6959
www.vividpublishing.com.au

National Library of Australia cataloguing-in-publication data:
Creator: Martin, Geraldine F., author.
Title: Della Mortika : Circus of Secrets / Geraldine F Martin.
ISBN: 978-1-922565-82-2 (paperback)
Series: Della Mortika steampunk adventures ; Bk. 3.
Target Audience: For primary school age.
Other Authors/Contributors:
            Martin, Paul J., illustrator.
            Martin, Marisa, illustrator.
Subjects: Fantasy fiction.
            Missing children--Fiction.
Dewey Number: A823.4

**To order further copies or to contact the author, please
visit www.vividpublishing.com.au/dellamortika3**

ACKNOWLEDGEMENTS

THANK YOU TO ALL MY FRIENDS, FAMILY AND COLLEAGUES WHO HELPED TO BRING THIS, THE THIRD NOVEL IN THE DELLA MORTIKA SERIES, TO FRUITION. IN PARTICULAR, MARISA WHO PAINTS LOVELY CHARACTERS AND WHO MANAGES TO MAKE EVERYTHING LOOK BETTER THAN BEFORE AND PAUL WHO AS USUAL CAME UP WITH SOME AMAZING DRAWINGS. THANKS ALSO TO SONJA CHANDLER WHO EDITED THE MANUSCRIPT.

PREVIOUSLY...

AFTER LEAVING THE UK IN 1888, THE DELLA MORTE SISTERS ARE SEPARATED FROM THEIR PARENTS - WHO ARE NOW PRESUMED DEAD BY EVERYONE BUT THE SISTERS. THEY FIND THEMSELVES IN AN ORPHANAGE AND ARE ADOPTED BY THE MALEFIC TWINS WHO TURN OUT TO HAVE EVIL INTENTIONS.

ABIGAIL, BEATRIX & ZARAH ESCAPE FROM THE LIBRARY OF WONDER WITH A NEW FRIEND CHARLIE BUTTONS AND A YOUNG MAN THEY MET IN GAOL CALLED MITCHELL O'CONNOR.

THE GIRLS HAVE A FIGHT OVER A HANDSOME SOLIDER NAMED LT PASHA DIMITRIKOV, WITH BEATRIX DOING DASTARDLY THINGS TO ABIGAIL...BUT AS IT IS WITH SIBLINGS, ALL IS SOON FORGIVEN.

NOW THE SISTERS FIND THEMSELVES STOWING AWAY WITH THE CIRCUS WHILE THEY CONTINUE TO SEARCH FOR THEIR PARENTS...

❧

Della Mortika - Circus of Secrets is the third novel in the Della Mortika Steampunk Series. Also in this series:

Novel 1. Della Mortika - Voyage to the Antipodes
Novel 2. Della Mortika - Library of Wonder
The award winning short animated film **Della Mortika - Carousel of Shame**

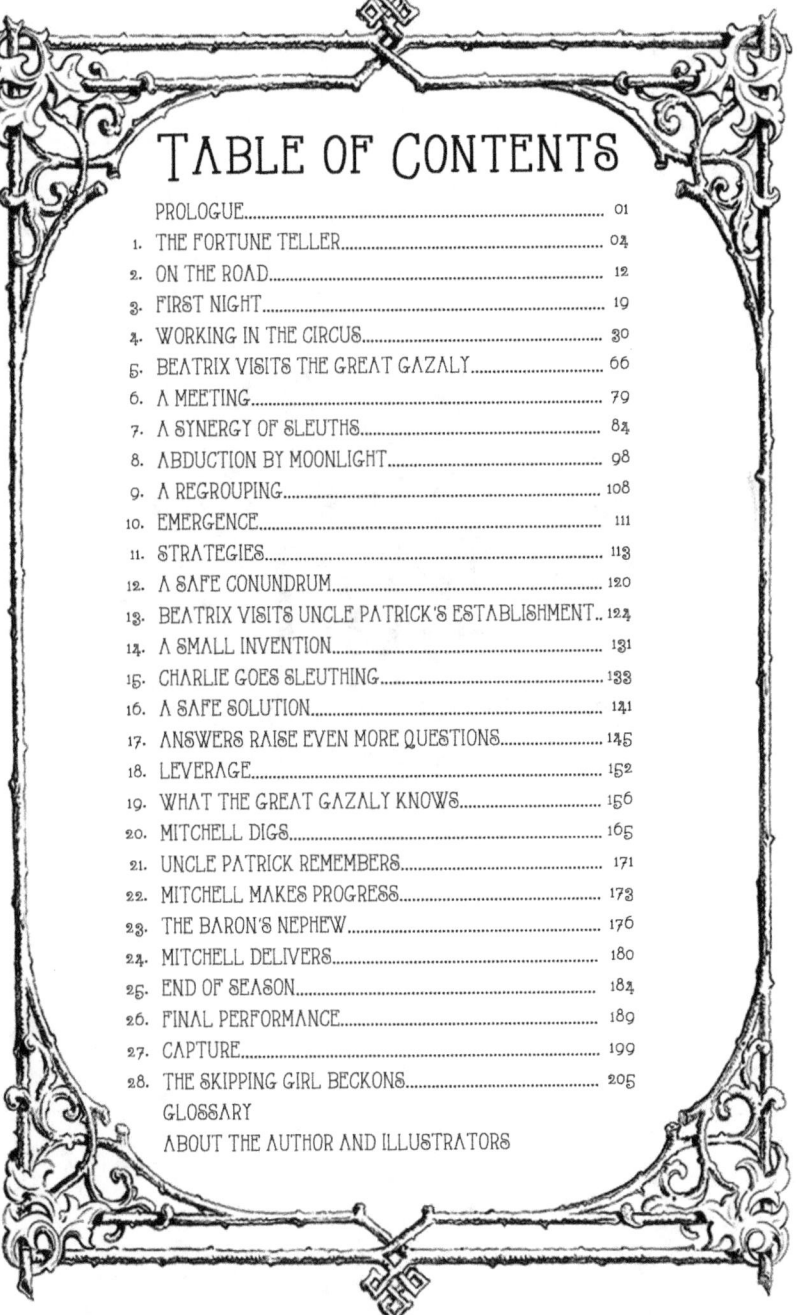

TABLE OF CONTENTS

Prologue

The Baron Ernst von Barbicon was hunched over a letter that he was reading intently through his pince-nez perched precariously on his thin aristocratic nose. He was leaning slightly to the right to catch the very best light from the kerosene lamp on the table next to his armchair. A small fire was casting shadows across his face and his mouth was moving convulsively. The grumbling started deep in his throat and his body began to tremble until he was quivering like a volcano about to erupt.

Suddenly he cried out, "A cataclysmic shower of fire and brimstone on their heads! May they all explode into a thousand speckles of ash! I will not let them get away with this!"

With that, he stood up abruptly and threw the letter into the fire. He watched it burn, his fists opening and closing in time with his breathing.

"Now, now, my dear. What has put you into such a fury?" asked a soft voice from the chair on the opposite side of the fire.

The Baron was still breathing hard, but at the sound of the voice his shaking began to subside and his breathing to slow.

Without turning from the fire, he said, "Ah, Lydia. The Society of Inventors has rejected my application for reinstatement for the fifth time."

Lydia turned her brown eyes upon him and said quietly, "Yes. I can see how that would upset you."

Baroness von Barbicon was recovering from her most recent bout of the consumption and still retained an unbecoming pallor to her skin and a debilitating weakness in her limbs. She had been afflicted with a chronic form of the disease since she was in her twenties. It waxed and waned and took its toll on her body. She was extremely thin and a little hunched over. Her mind, however, was as quick and as full of the glow of ambition as that of her husband.

"So, my dear. We will continue with our plan?" Lydia queried, her eyes focused on her husband's back as piercing as sharpened rail spikes.

The Baron turned slowly towards her; glared into her eyes with his own steely determination; and nodded as he said slowly, "Oh, yes, my dear Lydia; we will most certainly continue with our plan!"

The Fortune Teller

February 1889

"Come forward; don't be shy. Ask the question your heart most desires to have answered! And I, the Great Gazaly, will answer your questions."

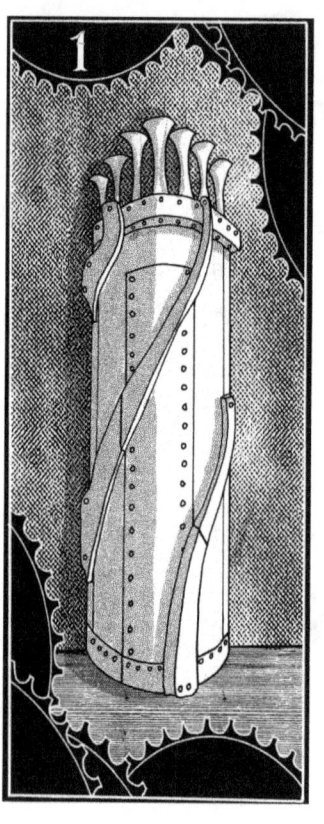

The crowd was still recovering from the thrilling sight of the tent's arrival. The occasion had begun with the calliope master playing. He had started with a soft piece of mysterious music which began to draw the crowd from Sideshow Alley and even from outside the circus grounds. The calliope was positioned outside and to the left of the entry to the Big Top.

The music had started to build and was giving rise to a feeling of anticipation and tension among the crowd. Some years ago, the master had had fitted two extra mechanical arms to enable him to amplify the impact of his music. Now, he brought all his arms into play. The music escalated. Something was about to happen. The crowd could feel it.

Under the music the crowd could hear a rhythmic sound they had not heard before. It seemed to be coming from behind the Big Top. They gasped as they saw the source of the sound rising slowly above the roof. Rotating blades were lifting something into the sky. The crowd was fixated on what the blades carried. Revealing itself was what appeared to be a circus tent. Not an ordinary tent, but one with working gears and a small steam engine underpinning the structure itself which was covered in billowing canvas tent walls. It was square in shape with a vaulted top culminating in a rotunda, out of the centre of which a pole supporting the rotating blades rose with great majesty.

The tent rose high in the sky and tipped its front end towards the crowd in greeting. It then circled the Big

Top, swooping lower as it travelled over the crowd. The crowd was enthralled, pointing and laughing in awe of this amazing sight.

A circular area outside the ticket box to the Big Top had been fenced off prior to the show beginning and eventually the tent stopped flying directly over the fenced area. Slowly, the tent sank to the ground and the blades stopped rotating. The crowd pressed closer and closer, trying to be the first to see what was going to happen next. Minutes passed, then the crowd gasped to see question marks of smoke shooting out of the top of the central pole and the words above the entrance to the tent lighting up with gas-infused energy –

THE GREAT GAZALY AND HIS VERITABLE VORTEX OF FUTURE FORCES.

Who was this? What was this? The crowd murmured, turning to each other, asking the questions.

Suddenly, the entrance curtains opened and out stepped a small man followed by a young woman slightly to his right. Behind them emerged a large glass cylinder that stopped in front of the now closing entrance curtains. The cylinder appeared to hover about two feet above the ground.

The Great Gazaly was a round, cheery-looking, middle-aged man dressed in the manner known as "industrial chic". His hat was a modified bowler complete with brass goggles (the eyes needing protection from the swirling future forces he was about to encounter). His tailcoat was black with rusted trims along the pockets and front. Under his coat he sported a magnificently embroidered waist coat and pristine white ruffled shirt. His trousers were black and his boots were topped with spats to his knees done up with brass buttons.

He stood outside his tent, spruiking his talents to a growing crowd of Melbournians. It was his job to gather customers together and astound them with his predictions of the future, prior to the opening of the show in the Big Top.

"Come forward; don't be shy! Ask the question your heart most desires to have answered!

"And I, the Great Gazaly, will answer your question!"

The Great Gazaly was the circus's fortune teller and a showman. He was popular with the customers, taking their questions about their future and delivering his predictions through an impressive display of skill and credibility.

He would listen to their questions and retire to his Veritable Vortex of Future Forces, which was the cylinder of glass that had emerged from his tent, where he could be observed sitting with his eyes closed in a swirl of mist and flashing lights. Atop the cylinder sat a circle of trumpet-like shapes reaching out into the air. The funnels circled faster and faster drawing in strange mists that no one had noticed before. He placed a helmet-like device on his head upon which sat a miniature circlet of funnels which sucked in smaller portions of the mist. When the swirling and lighting ceased, he would remove the helmet, step out of the Vortex and stand, legs wide, head back, thus giving himself time to recover from his recent arduous ordeal. He would then deliver his predictions in a voice of authority. He was rarely able to say with one hundred percent certainty that something would occur, but he could predict with some level of certainty that it would or would not. Often, he was right. Sometimes he was wrong, but not often. He was a great drawcard and the circus owner, the Ringmaster, felt gratified to have secured his contract.

The Antipodean Circus of Oddities and Amazing Sights had been in Melbourne for four months. The circus would stay another month or so before moving on to other Victorian regional centres. It was February and summer was still hanging on. It had been a hot summer, dry and windy and the circus staff were looking forward to the cooler weather of the coming autumn. The Great Gazaly was too professional to show any of this tiredness and he continued to encourage people to ask him questions.

The Great Gazaly had an assistant, the young woman who had emerged from the tent with him. She appeared to be about sixteen years of age and was dressed in a long plaid skirt, a blouse with a high ruffled neck and buttoned up boots. Over the blouse she wore a tight-fitting jacket. The whole outfit bespoke a conservative approach to her attire in one so young. Atop her brown hair with its glorious golden highlights perched a tiny top hat adorned with a feather. Her demeanour was calm and welcoming.

Her job appeared to be to meet and coordinate prospective questioners before they were ushered into the presence of the great man himself. Now she was talking to a young couple. She questioned them, quietly writing a few words in her notebook. Finally, she motioned the young man and woman, who was heavily pregnant, toward the fortune teller.

"Ah, yes, yes, come forward", the Great Gazaly said warmly, encouraging the couple to ask their question.

"I am about to give birth," said the young woman. "We want to know the colour of our baby's eyes."

"I am intrigued that you would need to know this," he said taking notes. "But of course, I will be able to tell you once I have had time to consult the Veritable Vortex of Future Forces. Do you happen to know the colour of the eyes of the child's grandparents?" He took further notes. He handed the notebook to his assistant and followed the usual routine.

Once he had emerged from the Vortex and had recovered sufficiently to speak, he pronounced, "I predict the child's eyes will most certainly be brown. There is a tiny possibility of blue, but this will very probably not happen."

The young parents looked relieved and thanked the Great Gazaly profusely for his prediction before they sank back into the crowd. The great man looked after them with a puzzled look before they were swept from his mind by the arrival of the next seeker of fortune. He had many predictions to make before the show opened in the Big Top.

On The Road

4 Months earlier – 20 October 1888

It was four months earlier that the Della Morte sisters and their friends, Mitchell O'Connor and Charlie Buttons, had jumped aboard the calliope vehicle and joined the slow-moving circus parade and they had been well and truly caught up in circus fever.

The spectacle of The Antipodean Circus of Oddities and Amazing Sights on the move was magnificent. It was led by two huge steel-plated elephants powered by their own internal steam engines which once stoked could power the giant pachyderms for over an hour, long enough to lead the parade to the site in Bourke Street where the circus would set up for the next four months and provide entertainment, mystery and exotic intrigue to the denizens of Melbourne. Atop the elephants sat their handlers all decked out in colourful Indian garb. The elephants themselves were decorated with beautiful silks and tassels. Every five minutes the handlers would pull on one of several levers arranged in front of the howdah in which they sat, and the elephants would raise their trunks and trumpet with deafening gusto.

The musicians followed the elephants, playing marching songs to which a squad of smartly dressed marching girls kept in step. In front of the squad was a small dynamo of a majorette who twirled her silver-plated baton and performed a varied and exciting range of gymnastic movements – not once dropping the baton. She was always moving, always busy and hypnotic to watch. This was Suzette, a member of a famous German family of gymnasts, who had come to Australia to seek her fortune. She was a popular attraction and greatly valued by the circus owners.

In contrast to the lithe and sprightly Suzette, next came Brutus, The Strongest Man in the World. He was an enormous and heavily muscled figure who strutted down the street wearing a top hat, a loin cloth and Roman sandals. His feet were wide apart as the muscles in his thighs would not allow his feet to meet. He held a lead ball the size of a watermelon above his head as easily as if it were a balloon. He turned his upper body from side to side acknowledging the applause of the crowd. Brutus had visited Melbourne last year with a rival circus and had gathered a huge following. The people admired not only his strength but also that his performances pitted his prowess against machines which were different each time. This crowd loved him.

The bulk of the parade was made up of two trains of ten carriages pulled by two steam locomotives. Tethered to each steam locomotive was a hot air balloon, which trailed banners advertising the circus and its attractions. In the basket of each were the balloon pilots and their families complete with horns and clappers. They waved and encouraged the people of Melbourne who were drawn to the route of the parade to come to the circus and have the 'experience of a lifetime'.

Each carriage was made up of three parts. At the

bottom sat a caravan-type structure, which provided housing for the many performers and back-stage workers who travelled with the circus. Each caravan was brilliantly decorated with the details and talents of the tenants, such as The Mighty Tyrone – The Human Punching Bag, Madame Chong – Costumier and Milliner to the Rich and Famous and The Great Bluey – Tight Rope Walker Extraordinaire. The top two sections would fold out when they reached their destinations and form the infrastructure of the circus proper. For the most part the caravans were empty as the occupants walked beside their carriages handing out the boiled black-and-white lollies known as 'humbugs' to the children lining the street.

The clowns were especially active, equipped as they were with their 'springers' which were springs, made of steel, a recently available material in the colony, attached to their oversized shoes. The springers were especially manufactured for them by the boot maker and the blacksmith, both of whom accompanied the circus. The skills required to perform in the springers took time to acquire but when the Clownspringers, as they had become known, had mastered them they brought a new freedom to the previously land-locked pranks and jokes they were able to perform. Once on the go at full pace, it often took quite some time to slow down. They frequently engaged in competitions between themselves about how high and far they could jump. However, one misstep could be catastrophic and some fatalities had even occurred. The greatest Clownspringer in this circus was Misery, famous for his hangdog make-up and his springer gymnastics. There had been a recent rumour that Misery was secretly developing an act that would combine springing with the high wire.

The parade had ended in a vacant lot on the corner of Bourke and Spring Streets and the construction of the extravaganza had begun. Firstly, the carriages were brought in a predetermined order into an oval where they would perform a dual purpose. The top section of the carriages would then open up on the inside of the oval to form seating and the base of the big tent. The middle section would unfold outward to form the framework for the stalls of Sideshow Alley which would run around the exterior of the tent. The caravans stood between these two functions. A team of roustabouts took under an hour to ensure the seating and the stalls were secured before they turned their attention to the erection of the big tent which was supported by two giant poles and canvas covering. The canvas was secured around the perimeter to the base of the carriages supplemented by stakes driven into the ground and guide ropes. The steam-powered elephants did the heavy work and the entire structure was finished before the sun set at 9 o'clock that night. Another group of simple caravans was sharing another space some way from the big tent. In other areas of the site some circus amusements, which had been unpacked at the same time as the big top, were being assembled. These included a small roller coaster, a carousel and several other small rides and activities.

Small fires began to spring up around the outsides of the stalls and caravans. The carnies were setting about their usual nightly tasks of cooking the evening meal and putting the children to bed. The smoke from the fires filled the air and drifted upwards towards the starry sky. People could be heard talking and singing softly. This was the social time of the day for the carnies, a nightly routine to which they looked forward during their workdays. Today had been especially tiring, parading and setting up was hard work. Eventually, the carnies themselves smothered their fires and retired to their caravans. The show opened on the morrow and they needed their sleep.

Five figures stood together in the darkness looking over the scene. Now that all was quiet and the rough and tumble of the day was completed, they looked at each other.

"What do we do now?" asked one small voice.

First Night

That first night the three Della Morte sisters and their friends Mitchell and Charlie found themselves in a dark and shadowy place, the only sounds the murmuring of the carnies putting out their fires and preparing to take to their beds for a well-earned night's sleep.

The friends crept quietly around the caravans careful not to call unwanted attention to themselves. The girls held hands and Zarah led the way. Mitchell and Charlie brought up the rear peering into the shadows looking for any signs of danger.

Eventually, they reached the entrance to the Big Top and managed to climb through into the now empty and very, very dark showplace. Zarah felt rather than saw her way through the entrance tunnel and into the back area of the first set of seats. They went in a little further and settled in an area large enough to accommodate all five of them. Mitchell took out his flint box and a small flame illuminated the space giving their faces unfamiliar and uneasy expressions.

"Looks like we'll be safe here for tonight anyway," whispered Mitchell.

Abigail sat down with her back to the wall between the seats and the side of the caravan to which the seats were attached. She gathered Beatrix to her right side and Zarah to her left and pulled them close.

Beatrix was weeping softly. "Abi, I'm so scared," she managed between sobs. "I want to go home and I want my mother."

"Sshh, Bea. I miss her too. This will have to do for tonight," Abigail said quietly. "We must be ready for tomorrow, whatever that brings."

The five of them had not thought any further than getting as far away from the burning Library of

Wonder as they could earlier that day. They had no blankets, no food and, as far as they knew, no friends.

It was still warm and it was some time before any of them managed to fall asleep. But sleep they did.

That was until daylight began to seep through the holes in the canvas of the Big Top and a voice roared from somewhere in the dim light around them.

"Well, well! What do we have here? Stowaway sprockets, by the looks of it!"

The young people were startled into wakefulness. Zarah jumped to her feet, as did Charlie, to face the intruder. Mitchell's first impulse was to run. He was good at that; but after looking over at the sisters he resisted and stayed as still as he could. Abigail rose to her feet, pulling Beatrix with her who was clinging to her sister's arm as if her life depended upon it.

Staring at them was the smallest man they had ever seen. He was dressed in a perfectly fitting suit with an immaculate white shirt and a red tartan bow tie.

On his head he wore a little hat that was fitted with a brightly coloured feather. He wore this hat at a jaunty angle. His face was made up and he looked like a ventriloquist's doll brought to life, the lipstick making the size of his mouth match the loudness of his voice.

He turned his head and roared over his shoulder, his finger pointing directly at the stowaways, "Hey boss, look'ee what I just found!"

At this, a pair of black shiny boots appeared beside the small figure. The body wearing the boots bent over and a face appeared and squinted at the young stowaways through his pince-nez.

After a second or so, he beckoned and said with something like weariness in his voice, "Right, out you come! Let's get a look at you and see what you have to say for yourselves. Come on, come on, today is a busy day. Our first performance is in three hours. I don't have all day to deal with the likes of you."

"You heard the Ringmaster. Hurry up! Hurry up!" called the small man, his huge voice echoing in the empty Big Top.

Slowly the stowaways made their way into the open space at the centre of the Big Top. The small man hassled them along and lined them up to face the Ringmaster. By now a crowd of carnies had gathered in the entrance tunnel and were quietly talking amongst themselves and pointing at the friends.

"Right, you scallywags, what are you doing hiding in my fine establishment? Eh?"

The friends all started to talk at once, but the Ringmaster put up his hand to stop the onslaught. "Stop it; stop that blathering. You make my head ache as though my thinking pistons were rusty. One at a time. You first", he said pointing at Abigail.

Abigail glanced at her sisters before she spoke, nodding and reassuring them.

"Sir, we apologise for trespassing in your tent last night, but we truly have nowhere to stay. The home where we had been held against our will burned down yesterday and when we saw your parade we jumped aboard the calliope machine trolley to escape."

The Ringmaster's eyebrows had been climbing slowly up his forehead. "Really, he said, "held against your will, a fire, escape!!" All five of the heads nodded. "Really." He looked over at the crowd at the door. "Well friends it looks like we have a new act – Tall Tales from the Mouths of Babes." The crowd laughed appreciatively.

"You know what I think? Whatever you say happened to you is your business. If you truly have nowhere to go, I can offer you employment in return for board and accommodation. No wages, mind. I can't afford that."

"Excuse me, sir," said Mitchell. "I do have a place to stay and I think my uncle's ur, um, employees have found me and are ready to escort me home." At that, two women Trudie and Rosalie– moved towards Mitchell. Each took one arm and marched him out of the tent. He did not resist. He had grown to know it was no use to fight this pair. Mitchell looked over his shoulder at the sisters, mouthing, "I'll be back."

"The remaining four of us are indeed homeless, Sir," said Abigail, "and would appreciate any help you can give us. My name is Abigail. I am a scholar and cryptologist. Beatrix is a seamstress. Zarah is the best example of a young engineer you could hope to find. And Charlie, well, Charlie needs to be kept as far as possible from any buttons he might push; he finds them irresistible."

"If this young lady describes herself as a cryptologist, then she would certainly have the kind of mind to be of great assistance to me in developing new directions with my Veritable Vortex of Future Forces," called a voice from the back where a very short, round middle-aged man was standing.

The Ringmaster nodded towards Abigail, "What do you think of that, young lady?"

Abigail gazed at this man she would get to know as the Great Gazaly and said, "His words intrigue me. I would be happy to be of assistance with his, vortex, did he say?"

"Excellent," shouted the relieved Ringmaster, "that

is settled then."

Another voice called from the left, "I too could use some help with my performance as I have been on my own since my wife died. That young lady would suit." He nodded towards Abigail. This was the Miraculous Memory Man.

"That's two of you with your hands up," marvelled the Ringmaster. "You three sort things out tomorrow. Miss, please visit Professor Landers tomorrow morning and the Great Gazaly in the afternoon. I suggest a half day with each of these should keep you very busy."

"And I'll take the seamstress," piped up a small Chinese woman. "With my workload, and my lack of steam-powered assistance, I need all the help I can get. Her name is Beatrix, yes?"

"Quite so, Madame Chong."

"The young one is an aspiring engineer, you say?" asked a woman with curly red hair and dressed in masculine attire. She was wiping her hands with an oily rag and had smeared oil in her hair when she had pushed it away. "I'll take her. Report to the Mechanical and Entourage Shed at dawn tomorrow," she called over her shoulder to Zarah as she hurried away.

"The other young one can come with me. He looks like he can handle the mini acrobat training and he will find it hard to find a button within cooee," called an athletic young man in cream singlet and shorts, a whistle around his neck.

"Well, thank you Lenny," said the Ringmaster. He turned to the young people. "There, we have managed to gain you employment. I expect you to work hard, mind. I have a spare small caravan. You can all sleep in there and you can cook for yourselves or get your food from the victuals van. Now off you go, I have work to do."

The sisters and Charlie stayed in the Big Top until all the circus people had left.

"Well," said Abigail. "What do we all think? Should we stay here a while with the circus or do you think we should return to the Skipping Girl Home and the Boys' Asylum? Or should we look for somewhere else?"

Zarah was jumping up and down with excitement. "Oh, I want to stay here. What an adventure!" she cried.

"Me too," said Charlie. "Anywhere is better than going back to the Asylum."

Abigail looked at Beatrix and asked, "What about you, Bea? What do you want to do?"
Beatrix was pale and fighting back her tears. "I want to go home. This place is horrible; it's too hot;" she sobbed, "and I want my mother."

"Yes, Bea, we all want to find our parents and I think we would have more freedom here with the circus to look for them. I also think the circus is a much more interesting place to work than the Great Laundry. So, shall we stay here for now?" asked Abigail.

A yes from Zarah and a yes from Charlie. Abigail looked at Beatrix who, still sniffing, mumbled, "I suppose so, if we have to, sniff."

"Good, that's decided then. We start work in the circus tomorrow," concluded Abigail.

The sisters and Charlie spent the rest of that day settling into their caravan and the circus. Other than choosing their beds there was not much to do in the caravan as they had only the clothes they were wearing when they fled the Library of Wonder. After this they wandered around the circus grounds, getting to know the layout of their new home and thinking about what tomorrow would bring.

Working In The Circus

The next morning Abigail woke and wondered where she was. She looked around and saw there were three other occupants with her in a small caravan. Then she remembered. They had been taken in by the circus and given this van to live in. They all four now had jobs in the circus. The next thought Abigail had was of her parents, Edgar and Celeste Della Morte, and how much she missed  them. She determined anew that she would look after her sisters and friends until they were reunited with their mother and father.

"Wake up, everyone," Abigail called out cheerfully.

"Today is our first day working in the circus and we can't be late."

Abigail

In what Abigail thought of as 'The Slave Auction' of yesterday morning, Professor Henry Landers, the Miraculous Memory Man, had requested that Abigail assist him in training for and demonstrating his amazing ability to remember facts, songs, poems, lists, dates and so on. He needed a replacement for his previous assistant, his wife, who had recently died. Abigail was to meet with him this morning.

She arrived early on that first day to see the Professor waiting for her outside the door to his tent. Abigail was a tall young woman, with long sleek brown hair with golden highlights. She wore a long plaid skirt and white blouse with a high collar. Although the day was hot she had chosen to don her best – and only – jacket for the occasion.

"Good morning, Professor," Abigail said as she approached him. He bowed formally before he spoke. "Good morning, my dear. I apologise that I have forgotten your name."

Abigail looked surprised.

"Ha, ha, Miss Abigail. That's just my little joke. Welcome to my tent. I am looking forward to working with you," he said as he held open the flap for Abigail to enter.

Relieved, Abigail followed the Professor into the tent. The Professor was middle-aged with a tall string bean of a figure. His favourite form of dress was a black suit and a stovepipe hat. He was a great admirer of Abraham Lincoln and had been in mourning since the day of the assassination of the President of the United States in 1865. Once seated at a small table with two chairs, the Professor poured the tea he had prepared and offered a small plate of biscuits to Abigail. As Abigail sipped her tea, he explained his work to her.

"As you know, Abigail, I am known as the Miraculous Memory Man. My job is to remember things. I wasn't born with a great memory and certainly not a photographic memory. No, no, no! I trained myself in several techniques that allow me to convince the circus public that I can remember anything they like to throw at me. It has been hard work and I am continually tested."

"Would you be able to teach me some of these techniques, Professor," asked Abigail. "My memory is quite good, but the only technique I know is to repeat something until I can remember it verbatim."

"Yes, well, that is a reasonably good way for students to learn, but if you want to be an expert there are several more efficient methods you could use," replied the Professor. "You know yesterday morning when you were discovered I admired your ability to speak on behalf of your friends and could see that you were intelligent and confident. I had thought you would make a good partner in my performance, interacting with the audience and making me look good."

Abigail raised her eyebrows at this. "Well it would be easy for you," the Professor continued hurriedly. "Clap when they need to clap; ooh and aah at my incredible feats; look scared when it seems I might not know the answer. You know the kind of thing," the Professor finished looking at her hopefully.

"I see," remarked Abigail. "I could do all that I suppose. But my interest would lie in learning some of the techniques you referred to."

"If you are truly interested, I could certainly teach you, I suppose. You could study during the mornings as well as practising our performance for the evening."

Abigail nodded her agreement and thus was forged a mutually beneficially partnership.

"We'll start with some simple mnemonics and work our way up to the memory palace – the jewel in the crown of memory techniques," assured the Professor as he ushered her out of the tent. "We'll start tomorrow morning, first thing."

Having left Professor Landers tent Abigail looked about for someone to provide her with directions to the tent of the Great Gazaly.

Out of the corner of her eye Abigail saw that Suzette

was practising throwing her silver baton into the air and catching it. Abigail approached Suzette and asked her for help. Suzette didn't stop practising and didn't speak but she did point Abigail in the direction she should take. As Abigail turned away, Suzette caught her baton and stood watching Abigail's back as she walked towards her destination.

****

Yesterday morning, the Great Gazaly, the circus fortune teller, had also requested that Abigail be his assistant, helping him to develop new directions for his Veritable Vortex of Future Forces. She arrived at his tent just after midday on that first day to talk with him about his request and stood outside the entrance.

The flaps of the canvas walls of the tent were locked with an elaborate piece of fine machinery custom-made for the Great Gazaly himself. To the left of the entrance stood a tall table solidly fixed into the ground. Atop the table was a set of gears and a crank handle. "Crank the handle three times clockwise to alert the Great Gazaly of your arrival" was written on a sign attached to the bottom of the device.

Abigail took a deep breath and turned the handle three times in a clockwise direction. She looked up and listened, but she could hear nothing. A she was trying again a great roar sounded from within the tent and there was rustling at the lock to the entrance flaps.

"I heard you the first time," shouted the Great Gazaly as his face emerged between the flaps. "What the Charles Dickens do you want at this time of the day?"

Abigail stepped back in fright and was altogether too shocked to speak.

The Great Gazaly focused his eyes upon her pale face and his voice softened. "Ah, it is you, young stowaway. I see I have frightened you. Please do not be afraid and come inside. We need to get to know each other."

He extended his hand and Abigail placed hers on it as he led her into the tent holding one of the flaps up for her. Once inside, he turned to relock the flaps increasing Abigail's nervousness.

"Please, Miss Abigail, do not fear. What I do here is very secret. If people learned of my methods my career would be in smithereens. Please sit."

Abigail looked around the space and observed a couple of chairs and a table. Light came through windows in the canvas roof which were equipped with covers to keep out the rain; but this day they were open. Abigail estimated that this part of the tent was partitioned off from much of the tent which, from the outside, looked large by circus standards.

"Now, Miss Abigail, tell me about yourself. How did you get into your present predicament?"

Abigail looked at his jolly open face and decided she could probably trust him with her story and explained the circumstances which had led to her and her sisters and friends, ending up at the circus.

The Great Gazaly, who, having been dealing with people most of his adult life, seemed to understand and nodded sympathetically. "You said last night that you were a cryptologist and a scholar. I am especially interested in your interest in cryptology and how wide that interest might have gone. Are you interested in mathematics? Have you ever heard of Ada Lovelace?"

Abigail's face brightened, "Oh yes! I have studied mathematics and I am a great fan of Ada Lovelace! I love her book and her work on algorithms is fascinating."

At this the Great Gazaly's face broke into a wide smile and he nodded appreciatively. He was a cousin of Charles Babbage, the engineer and inventor of the 'Difference Engine' which was a famous mechanical calculating machine developed in Britain. Cousin Charles had also designed his 'Analytical Engine' in the 1830s and had sold one of these to his cousin, the Great Gazaly whose real name was Lorenzo Mario Babbagio. He belonged to the Italian side of the family. He was also a mathematician, engineer and inventor in his own right. Lorenzo tinkered with his engine until he could make it calculate probabilities of outcomes based on inputs he placed in the machine using punched out cards. He saw an advertisement in the London Times for a fortune teller for a circus in the colony of Victoria, Australia. Being a man of adventure, he applied, was given the job and sailed out to Victoria bringing his Analytical and Probability Engine with him.

"I am delighted to hear this as I believe you have the potential to become as accomplished as Ada under my guidance and you could be a great asset to our field and to our circus performance," the Great Gazaly continued.

Abigail's eyes widened and she smiled. "Oh, sir", she said, "this is incredible. I couldn't have expected anything like this. This is very exciting for me."

The Great Gazaly considered her open and happy face for a few moments then he gestured to the curtains covering the entrance to the back of the tent. "I am about to put my trust in you. I can trust you, can't I, to keep what I am about to show you secret?"

Abigail's smile died a little and her eyes narrowed as she replied, "As long as it is not illegal or harmful in any way, I expect you can trust me to keep your secret."

"Of course, it's not illegal and I assure you no-one could possibly be hurt during this process. It's not only legal but innovative and exciting," the fortune teller assured her.

"Very well, then. On that condition, I will keep your secret," said Abigail.

Tthe Great Gazaly opened the curtains to the back of his tent to reveal a piece of machinery which took up a good part of the back of the tent. It was taller than he was and equipped with wheels. This was his Analytical and Probability Engine.

"You see, Abigail," stated the Great Gazaly, "I really do not foresee the future, I simply calculate the probabilities of something happening or not."

Abigail held her hands over her mouth to stifle her scream. Once she had absorbed what he had said, her mind started whirling with questions. Was the Great Gazaly a sham, a charlatan? How could this be?

The Great Gazaly recognised Abigail's reaction and rushed to reassure her he was simply a scientist and engineer who was using today's technology to present data in a form that his customers would accept and understand.

Abigail, a true scientist at heart, felt uneasy about this concept. "But the technology deserves recognition. You deserve recognition for your abilities to make the technology work," she managed to say. "Hiding behind the front of a fortune teller undermines your integrity and dupes your gullible customers."

"Ah, Abigail, there are dark forces at work that you do not understand."

"What forces?"

"I am not at liberty to say. But my safety depends on the secret staying just that, secret."

"So, the Veritable Vortex of Future Forces is just window dressing to deceive your customers into believing that you can foretell the future," Abigail mused to herself.

"And what part am I to play in this subterfuge?" she then asked him.

"I will teach you all I know about writing algorithms for my engine and you shall become expert at it, the Ada Lovelace of the Antipodes. It is a great opportunity. But I must again swear you to secrecy before I can make you the offer."

Abigail sat looking at the Great Gazaly for several seconds before she nodded and said, "As I said previously, I will keep your secret and I will accept your offer, but on the further condition, that once these 'dark forces' have lost their hold on you that you will emerge from hiding behind the Veritable Vortex of Future Forces and step into the light. Deal?"

"Deal," agreed the Great Gazaly and they shook hands on it.

After that first day Abigail spent her mornings with the Miraculous Memory Man and her afternoons with the fortune teller.

Abigail found working with Professor Landers easy and enjoyable. For his performances she had Madam Chong make her a black suit and little top hat to match the Professor's and she submerged herself into her role of crowd activator. She found that the people in the audience responded well to her, especially when she laughed and jollied them along. She had been a serious girl all her life and this was an outlet for her heretofore hidden inner joy. During the mornings she conscientiously studied the memory techniques that the Professor was teaching her. She was especially good at mnemonics. For remembering the classification of living things, she made up "King Pharaoh Cast Out the Family Goat into the Sea". The first letter of each of the capitalised words represented the hierarchy of living things: K=Kingdom, P=Phylum, C=Class, O=Order, F=Family, G=Genus and S=Species.

In the afternoons with the fortune teller a partnership based on scholarship and trust was played out. Abigail absorbed all that the Great Gazaly could teach her and she was soon designing her own algorithms for the engine. Two months later she started assisting 'the GG', as she called him, in his fortune-telling performances. Two weeks after that he stopped checking her work and allowed her to run the machine on her own. His performances, if anything, increased in popularity with Abigail streamlining the process by questioning potential customers and then preparing the algorithms for the machine to inform the fortune teller. This was much faster than the Great Gazaly working on his own.

Her evenings were spent with her friends in their caravan. They told each other of their days and what was happening in various parts of the circus. One evening Beatrix came home looking quite excited.

"Abigail, I picked up a letter from Lieutenant Dimitrikov for you. Open it up and tell us what it says," Beatrix said holding out the letter to Abigail.

The sisters had met Lieutenant Pasha Dimitrokov during the time they were staying at the Skipping Girl Home for Homeless and Wayward Girls. Both Beatrix and Abigail had really liked him and there had occurred some unpleasantness between the sisters regarding who held his affections. But that is another story. Anyway, it turned out that the Lieutenant was really enamoured of Abigail and they pledged to write to each other when he had been posted to Wodonga in the war between Victoria and New South Wales. The war was over the underground coal situated on the border between the colonies.

Abigail's eyes lit up when she took the letter from Beatrix.

"Oh," murmured Abigail, "I haven't heard from him for several months. I hope he has not been injured."

Abigail opened the letter and read it silently. She gasped at one stage and her hand covered her mouth.

"What is it?" asked Beatrix jumping up from her seat and leaning over her sister's shoulder trying to read what was written there. Abigail was silent and moved the letter away from her sister's gaze.

"What does he say. He's dead, isn't he? I knew it!" cried Beatrix, her eyes filling with tears.

"No, he's not dead, but he was injured," Abigail

assured her sister. "He was patched up and sent home to Melbourne several weeks ago." Abigail's eyes drifted over to the window. "I don't know where he lives and he hasn't been to see us. I hope he is alright."

Wiping away her tears, Beatrix brightened up saying, "I am sure he is and he'll come and visit us any day now."

"I hope you're right," said Abigail quietly, almost to herself.

Beatrix

Beatrix was less hopeful about what that first day might bring than Abigail. She had been pleased to find herself apprenticed to Madame Chong, a famous seamstress and milliner, but at the same time fearful of what she would be like to work for. Beatrix was thirteen years old and had no working experience at all. On the other hand, she loved sewing and designing and had a flair for colour, form and line and could see that this was a great opportunity for her, one which would not be given to many girls her age. So, she dressed and tried to brush her curly red-brown hair into submission. She worked hard to keep the butterflies in her stomach still and she made her way to Madam Chong's tent. She couldn't miss this tent as it was quite near their caravan and had a giant advertising board along the side featuring the smiling face of an oriental woman with a magnificent hat accompanied by glowing testimonials from famous clients under the heading Madame Chong's Magnificent Designs for Performers.

As she neared the entrance to the tent, she could see there was no bell or other apparatus to announce her arrival. So, she called out, "Madame Chong, it's Beatrix." There was no response. "Madam Chong, it's Beatrix," she tried again. Nothing. She took a very deep breath, smoothed her hair once again and pulled her jacket down. She then lifted the flap and stepped into the tent. Once her eyes had adjusted to the light in the tent, she saw towards the back a small figure leaning over a large table cutting fabric with the largest pair of shears Beatrix had ever seen. This was Madame Chong who was singing to herself. Beatrix could hear Chinese music playing in the background and the tent was filled with an aroma that Beatrix could not place. Beatrix called out once more, "Madame Chong, it's Beatrix. Good morning."

Madam Chong looked up from her work and beckoned Beatrix to come closer. Beatrix did so and could not help admiring the woman's bright pink silk straight gown. It was buttoned at the shoulder and Madame Chong called it a cheong san. She wore it loose over black trousers and had a jacket to wear with it when she went out. She wore platform shoes. She was descended from a Manchu family who did not bind the feet of their girls. Her long black shiny hair was wound into a bun with a beautiful pin to keep it in place. She was in her forties and reveled in the freedoms that living in Victoria provided her. She had lost her husband on the gold fields when they were younger. She had set about to learn English and eventually set herself up in business. She was a self-made woman.

"Welcome, Miss Beatrix. I am especially excited this morning to be playing the very latest in Peking Opera recordings on my Edison phonograph. The wax cylinder arrived yesterday and I haven't stopped playing it. It is called 'Farewell to Princess Yu' and is the story of a faithful consort who commits suicide rather than desert her master who is about to go into battle. It is so sad. Beautiful music isn't it?"

Beatrix had never heard such music before and it did not fall gently on her ears. However, she was a well brought up girl and agreed politely.

"Oh yes, beautiful indeed," she said moving closer to Madam Chong.

Madame Chong came forward to meet Beatrix and took her hands in hers.

"Well, my dear," began Madame Chong. "I am certainly glad to have you join me. I can certainly do with the help. There is so much cutting, stitching and ironing to do that I am completely stokered out. Everyone wants new costumes for the final performance which is in a few months' time. And what's more I hate the heat! I am tired! My back aches! And my fingers are sore," she continued on a rising crescendo until she looked closely at Beatrix's face and registered that she was a little taken aback by this outburst.

"Now, now, dear, don't mind me," she said softly. "We'll get along steampunkiously I'm sure."

Beatrix smiled and murmured, "I am sure we will. But I was hoping to use some of my own designs, you see ...."

Madame Chong immediately became serious and broke in on Beatrix with, "Yes, yes, all in good time. We have to make sure you can do the basics of sewing and millinery first. Work hard and you will earn my appreciation and when we have time you will get your chance to design. Just don't pistonag me, or you will be waiting much longer. I'd like you to get started in hemming those handkerchiefs I cut for the marching girls. They get so sweaty."

Beatrix sighed a little and picked up the handkerchiefs, needle, thread and scissors and found a quiet corner in which to sit and work. Madame Chong returned to her cutting out on the table.

For the next few months, Beatrix toiled beside Madame Chong doing the limitless small tasks that had to be done, such as ironing, mending and stitching, all the time striving to impress the seamstress with her eye for design. Somewhat unsuccessfully, it must be said.

Beatrix, however, was in her element. When the family had left London, four months ago, she had never thought that she would be working in the costume department of a circus! She had always had a flair for fashion and now, at the tender age of thirteen, that flair was as bright as ever. Just before they had left London, she had won a prize for her invention of a set of dress pattern templates at the London School of Invention where she and her sisters had been students.

Although saddened whenever she thought about her missing parents, her spirits would often rise the minute she walked into Madame Chong's tent. For here, the mysteries of the circus were laid out in the array of textiles and haberdashery that Madame Chong used to create the illusions of the many performances that the circus had presented to the public of the colonies for the past twenty years.

Beatrix loved to run her hands over the silks of the orient and the linens of Ireland. These were expensive fabrics, however, and used rarely and only for special occasions. Most common were homespun, cottons and hessian, for the genius of Madame Chong lay in her ability to turn these humble materials into a magnificent piece of art that lured the public into believing they really were in the presence of the military, or royalty or beings from other lands.

Zarah

Zarah knew she was expected at her designated workplace at dawn on that first morning. She rose early and dressed as she always did in cream pants and lace up boots. Her blouse was double breasted and brown with copper buttons. She wore her straight black hair with a fringe and one curl on the right side. On her head she always wore her goggles as she never knew when she would need them to protect her eyes from the soot of the Melbourne air. Her right forearm was encased in an arm brace in which she kept a cache of essential and surprising objects. She took little interest in her appearance. She found the world far too exciting for such fripperies as dresses and ribbons and dressed for comfort and practicality.

Just as the sun was rising for that first day Zarah approached the Mechanical and Entourage Shed. She stood in admiration of the size and imposing nature of the shed and wondered how it had travelled as part of the parade. What had the carnies done to make it portable and yet have transformed it overnight into the largest structure (apart from the Big Top) of the circus?

Zarah could make out the sounds of movement inside and suspected the day's work inside the shed was about to begin. She walked around the structure till she found an open door and walked quietly into the darkness. She could see nothing until a great shout ordered the opening of the huge front doors. This was the voice of authority, a feminine voice which Zarah quickly attributed to the now visible red-haired Chief Engineer. The shed flooded with the dawn light.

"You," the same voice shouted, "you're late!"

"No,...." Zarah started to say but was interrupted by

her new boss. "Ah, I see, a feisty little stowaway. Well, these elephants won't clean themselves. I want them gleaming by the end of the morning. Oily will show you what to do. So, pick up the pace and get to work!"

Zarah looked around and found only one face which was smiling at her. This face was black with smeared oil and had crooked teeth and just had to be the personage known as 'Oily'. He was elderly and moved as if he needed to apply his oil can to his joints to ease their stiffness. Dressed in overalls and an engineer's hat he could have stepped straight out of the driver's cabin of a steam locomotive.

Oily beckoned Zarah over to his place by the two giant elephants. "Don't mind the Chief, her squeak is worse than her grind. I'm getting a bit tight in the gaskets and find it hard to climb onto the elephants' backs. I'll give you a leg up and you can clamber aboard. Here, take this rag and rub Elsie's back and head until they gleam."

Zarah was overjoyed. To think that her first job was to work on the two fantastic elephants. She wondered when she would get her first glimpse of the inside workings of the huge machines.

From her vantage point atop Elsie, Zarah had a sweeping view of the shed. Most of the interior was open to accommodate the two great pachyderms. Around the edges were tables fitted with metal lathes and milling machines. This workshop produced all the gears, valves, tubes and gaskets needed to power and move the giants but also undertook repairs to all the mechanical and steam-powered machines that the circus relied upon. In one corner Zarah identified one metal worker producing the steel springs for the clowns to be attached to their shoes which allowed them to perform thrilling acts for the circus audiences.

Zarah was lost in her admiration of all she could see until Oily knocked on Elsie's leg and waved to her to get working. Zarah had never worked so hard. She rubbed round and round, up and down and side to side till every mark was erased and she could see her face beaming back at her.

She knew she was going to enjoy it there; and enjoy

it she did. She worked hard on establishing herself as an asset to the shed and to the Chief. She polished the elephants and swept the floor. She kept the workers and the Chief supplied with cups of tea and ran errands when needed. She watched and she learned, particularly on the workings of the elephants. She was small and could often help the mechanics with things that needed doing where they were too big or too lazy to reach inside the mechabeasts. She tightened nuts and bolts; she greased joints; and she studied the steam engines, levers and handles that controlled the movement of the great machines.

As with her sisters she did not forget her parents or stop missing them. She searched faces in the crowds and nipped along the Melbourne streets in her free time asking if anyone had any information about them or had seen them. She was a terrier and would never give up.

Mitchell

Mitchell woke that first morning in his own bed in his room behind his Uncle Patrick's business in the Market Square. His arms were bruised where Trudie and Rosalie had held him tightly when they had retrieved him from the Big Top on the preceding morning. Mitchell rubbed his arms and reflected on what had happened. How had they known I was there he thought to himself. He would not have much time to mull this over for as soon as he rose, dressed and was making his way to the offices of the business he was confronted by his uncle.

"Ah, boyo," called Patrick O'Connor as Mitchell walked to his desk. "I hear you were found with those Della Morte sisters at the circus that has just arrived in town."

"Yes," replied Mitchell. "Trudie and Rosalie arrived to escort me home early yesterday morning. You weren't here when we got back. May I ask where you were?" He continued hoping to fend off any further enquiries about his own doings.

"Now then, boyo, don't try to change the subject. I have warned you that your responsibilities are here and there is much for you to learn."

Mitchell sat down at his desk and commenced the day's work. The business was known as O'Connor's

Patents Pending and Realisation Office. Patents were important in Melbourne and the more you owned the wealthier you were. However, the process of having your patent licenced was not cheap and Patrick O'Connor was in the business of assisting young patent hopefuls to do just that. Mitchell had not yet fathomed how the whole thing worked, although he could see that his uncle was a very wealthy man. In Ireland, Patrick had been a tenant farmer and today he was what Mitchell called a flash toff – wealthy, well dressed and of high social status. Mitchell was very interested in how his uncle had pulled this off, but after several months he had learned very little about it.

Mitchell had learned to read and write from his mother, although he had not attended school very often as much work had to be done around the farm and Mitchell being the eldest had responsibilities. When the next child in line grew to be twelve, Mitchell was shipped off to the colonies to be trained by his uncle. For the previous few months he had been moving from one clerical task to the next. This week his work entailed opening the mail, stamping the date upon it and depositing it into the correct in-tray.

Mitchell had met the Della Morte sisters on their first day in Melbourne. They had been rescued from outside the Heads of Port Phillip Bay and brought to Port Melbourne and then to the Law Courts as abandoned and neglected children, and as orphans. That same day he had been apprehended by two floppers and deposited in the Holding Cells of the Law Courts where the sisters were also being held. He had been released into the custody of his uncle and the girls had been sent to the Skipping Girl Home for Wayward and Homeless Girls. He had met them several times after that culminating in the escape from the Library of Wonder and flight to the circus two nights ago.

Despite his uncle's trust in the powers of Trudie and Rosalie he was confident he had the skills needed to abscond as he had done several times before and seek the companionship of the sisters.

Mitchell did manage to visit the sisters and kept them apprised of what was happening in the wider world of Melbourne. Mitchell and his Uncle Patrick did not see eye-to-eye on a number of things and Mitchell often absconded from his uncle's office situated near the Market Square in North Melbourne. Invariably, Mitchell was retrieved by Trudie and Rosalie, or sometimes by the floppers of the Melbourne Constabulary. Floppers were the flying police powered by jet packs who patrolled the skies of the city. Floppers was the slang for flying coppers, with the word coppers slang for the constabulary. Since everyone knew that his friendship with the Della Morte sisters would draw him to them again and again, he had not proved hard to find over the past weeks.

Mitchell had a more specific reason for being drawn to the circus. That reason was a shy girl with unruly red-brown hair. There was something about her that appealed to him immensely. He and Beatrix had things in common. They both loved to dress well and look good. They were both intelligent, although their levels of education were different. Mitchell had street smarts and Beatrix was school educated. They were both far from home, although Beatrix was more homesick and a bit whingey. Mitchell, who normally fitted in easily with most people, felt a bit awkward when with the sisters. He came from an Irish farming family and they were from the English aristocracy. Mixing socially in Britain would not have been possible. Even out here in the colonies the old ways still held true for newcomers from the old country. But Beatrix wasn't like that. She was about his age and didn't show that she felt herself superior to him in any way. He really liked her for that and contrived to see her whenever possible.

Charlie

Charlie was delighted to be assigned to the acrobatic troupe. On that first day he arrived bright and early and was met by Lenny the troupe leader.

"Well, I'm pleased you turned up," Lenny remarked. "Are you happy to be with us? You look pretty fit and should be up to most of what the troupe is learning."

Charlie was the product of a mixed marriage between an Irishman and an Aboriginal girl. The family had moved down from the Snowy Mountains when he was very young. His story was a sad one. His father died from being run over by a horse-drawn carriage after a night at The Cog and Wheel and his mother took Charlie and proceeded to flee back to the mountains by train. Charlie, being Charlie, found a shiny red button alongside the emergency door of the train carriage they were on and pushed it. The door sprung open and Charlie fell out just outside Melbourne. His mother raised the alarm and a subsequent search by the Melbourne Constabulary failed to find the little boy. His mother gave up searching after a few months and returned to the Snowies believing her child dead and lost forever.

The child was anything but dead. He had fallen beside the tracks and rolled into a ditch dense with the weed Paterson's Curse. He was unhurt and being somewhat disoriented started walking along the tracks till he came to the Bacchus Marsh station. He climbed up onto the platform and joined a crowd of people and children waiting for the train to Melbourne. He mingled with the other children and rode the train till its journey ended at Flinders Street station whereupon he followed other people till he disappeared into the slums close to the station. Young orphaned children ran those streets living off what they could beg or steal using their street cunning. He managed to survive there for several months till he was picked up by the Floppers and delivered to the courts for being an abandoned and neglected child. An Irishman was in the court, having been on the lookout for his nephew since he had been last seen falling from a train, and informed the Magistrate that the child was in fact his nephew, Charlie O'Neill, and that he was prepared to take the child home to live with his wife and daughter, Nerida, in Richmond. The child's parents were deceased; his mother recently dying from the consumption and his father in a street accident. The Magistrate assigned Charlie to Mr O'Neill where he lived till he and his wife also succumbed to the ills of living in the slums of Richmond and died. Nerida, whom Charlie regarded as his sister, ended up in the Skipping Girl Home for Wayward and Homeless Girls in Abbotsford and Charlie in the Melbourne Boys' Asylum in South Melbourne. It was from there that he had been placed in the Library of Wonder where he met the Della Morte Sisters.

"Oh," sighed Charlie. "You have no idea how fit I am. I was the bike rider in the Library of Wonder generating the energy that made the machine work. Two 3-hour sessions per day for weeks on end. I'd say I was fit."

Charlie certainly looked fit. He was tall and lean for eleven. His skin was a lovely light brown colour and his hair was blonde. He had inherited the best from each of his parents – his dark skin and curly hair from his mother and his blonde hair and blue eyes from his father.

"That's an amazing piece of luck for us. Here, take those rags off and put these on. The rest of the troupe will be here soon, and we need to get to work." Lenny said as he handed over the troupe uniform of shorts, singlet and canvas shoes.

By the time the circus was gearing up for their final performance, Charlie had reached the point where he could tumble, climb and balance with the best of the child acrobatic troupe. He felt that finally he belonged somewhere; that he had a real purpose in life; that he was a real entertainer. He was looking forward to his first performance in the Big Top which was scheduled for that final performance at the end of February.

****

From that first day and for the following four months the girls and Charlie concentrated on their various tasks during the day as they each had much to do and much to learn. The sisters did not lose sight of the fact that their parents were missing, presumed by the authorities to be dead. They knew their parents were alive as they had watched them being scooped up after their flying ship had crashed into the sea. They had been swallowed by a leviathan, a huge zeppelin that had opened its mouth and closed over the little vessel in which their parents were trying to reach dry land. The Della Morte sisters and their friend Charlie settled into a routine of learning and performing with their allocated mentors. Mitchell spent his time between learning his uncle's business and escaping to visit the sisters and Charlie at the circus. Mitchell also managed to retrieve the girls' belongings from the home previously occupied by the owners of the Library of Wonder, which to this day had stood vacant following the destruction of the Library. The girls were especially appreciative as their meagre belongings included all they had in the colony of Victoria.

Beatrix Visits
The Great Gazaly

Forward four months to February 1889

"Ah! Miss Bea, at last you have arrived. Come over here. There is much to do today," called Madame Chong when she saw Beatrix standing over the silks and linens as she often did when she entered this tent.

"Good morning, Madame Chong," answered Beatrix, her curly mop of reddish hair bouncing attractively as she moved away from the silks toward the older woman, her hand sliding slowly down the fabric until just her fingertip still lingered on the edge. A second passed before she pulled her hand away and plonked down on the chair she usually occupied in the tent attached to Madame Chong's caravan. She pushed her mop of curls away from her face and adjusted her jacket.

Madame Chong was sitting at her treadle sewing machine, busily attaching a bright yellow tasseled trim to the red skirt of one of the marching girls' uniforms. Nodding her head to her right she indicated a stack of the same red skirts and said, "Those skirts need pressing. Stoke up the fire and fill the iron with coals and get to it. Please don't burn yourself and more importantly don't scorch the trim. Hop to it now."

She kept muttering under her breath as she sewed, "They can afford great steam engines for their fancy equipment but won't make allowance for a small engine for this tent. Selfish that's what they are and I'm not getting any younger."

Oblivious to the older woman's mutterings, Beatrix let out a dismayed, "Ironing! But Madame Chong, when am I going to be able to do some real designing?"

"I understand your impatience, my dear, but we have priorities. All will happen in due course. When you have finished the skirts, you can finish sewing the buttons for the Great Gazaly's jacket. He needs it for the final performance, and I want to make sure it fits."

Beatrix looked over to the mannequin standing to attention in the corner. It was adorned with a magnificent jacket in the Great Gazaly's usual military style. Its buttons were set down beside it ready for sewing on to the jacket. It was black with a mandarin collar and was designed to make the wearer look as slim as possible. This would suit the fortune teller beautifully as he had been struggling with his weight for decades.

"Yes, ma'am," Beatrix said as she smiled with anticipation, for she liked the fortune teller with his happy smile. Her sister Abigail had been working with him since the sisters had arrived, but she was a bit secretive about what that work entailed. She said it was confidential and was a closely guarded secret.

Beatrix really wanted to know the secret but so far had had no luck. This could be her chance!

Madam Chong had had many assistants over the years and knew the benefits of using incentives to coach the best work from others. She too smiled to herself and she continued to press the treadle rhythmically.

Beatrix had finished pressing the uniforms and was putting the finishes touches to the new skirt Madam Chong had made for Suzette, the head marching girl and gymnast, when the shadow of a man appeared on the side of the tent. Noticing the shadow, Madame Chong stopped pedalling her treadle sewing machine, looked over at Beatrix and said, "I think it's time for you to deliver the new jacket to the Great Gazaly, Miss Beatrix, if you wouldn't mind."

Miss Beatrix didn't mind at all. She was hot and bothered and couldn't wait to get out of the stifling tent and into the open air. She put the iron she was using on the stand to cool down and wiped her face and hands on her apron.

"Right away, Madame Chong. I'll cover it with a sheet to keep it clean and I'll be off."

Beatrix did so and picked up the covered jacket and placed it carefully over her arm.

The Great Gazaly was a good-humoured man who always enjoyed a chat and she was keen to see him this morning.

Just last week, Beatrix had asked him about the whereabouts of her parents. He had told her he didn't know where they were but, using the information she had given him, he was 85% sure they were still alive and 30% certain they were still in Australia.

So, Beatrix was happy to be on her way to visit him this morning. Working with Madam Chong and away from her sisters each day had increased her independence and she was feeling more confident in her own abilities. She still missed her parents and worried about them, but instead of being fearful and whingy she felt determined to find them.

Madame Chong's tent was on the opposite side of

the circus grounds to that of the Great Gazaly, so Beatrix had to pass by many of the caravans of the performers to reach his tent.

Coming towards her she could see Stromlo, the steam-powered man. He was made of steel plate and was fashioned as closely to a human figure as that material would allow. Inside beat the pistons of a small steam engine which cranked the gears and pulleys which allowed him to pull great weights. She reached him, he stopped, tipped his top hat which let out a shot of steam, bowed and put out his hand to shake hers. She politely gave him her hand which he shook.

"Good morning, Stromlo," Beatrix said to him.

"Good morning, Miss Beatrix," came from inside the head of Stromlo.

Beatrix wasn't shocked by this. She knew his secret. When he wasn't needed for heavy work, Stromlo Two was hidden inside allowing him to interact with the public, although he didn't speak to them because this would have destroyed the illusion.

Stromlo nodded his head, released her hand, stood up straight and continued on his way. He was attached to the Mechanical and Steam-Powered Entourage which included the elephants.

Further on Beatrix could hear the calliope player practising. He was playing a circus piece with fabulous abandon. There could be nobody in the circus still asleep with that going on. The music was cheerful and Beatrix found herself walking in time with the beat. Her mood elevated even more. The calliope player was Karl Nagy, Hungarian by birth and a former piano student of Franz Liszt. He had migrated to Victoria in the 1850s looking for gold. He didn't find any but by a stroke of luck won himself the calliope in a card game. With the instrument came the job at the circus. Karl threw himself into playing the music of his youth and with the aid of the two mechanical arms added to his body he played the most extravagant and difficult of pieces.

Beatrix passed her sister Abigail outside the caravan of the Miraculous Memory Man, Henry Landers.

Abigail spent her early mornings with Professor Landers and the rest of her day with the Great Gazaly. Beatrix didn't stop to chat as Abigail was concentrating hard with her eyes closed and a pack of playing cards in her hands. Her aim was to remember the order of the cards as shuffled by placing them into different rooms in the mansion in her head. When she attempted to recall them, she would walk through that mansion and retrieve the cards in the order that she had placed them there. Henry was a master at this technique and he was sharing his secrets with Abigail. In fact, Abigail was due to take a small part in the morning session a bit later.

As she walked closer to the Great Gazaly's tent, Beatrix could see the members of the mini acrobat troupe practising their tumbling routines. She smiled when she saw Charlie take his turn. When the others took one tumble, Charlie fitted in a double tumble. When Charlie saw Beatrix he waved and jumped up and down excitedly. Lenny, the troupe leader, soon put a stop to that and Charlie sat down with the others quickly. Lenny insisted on discipline in his team.

In the distance, Beatrix could see the Mechanical and Entourage Shed. She could make out one of the two elephants being driven out of the shed. On the back of the beast sat one of the elephant handlers and sitting in front was Zarah, obviously enjoying the experience.

Finally, Beatrix saw the Great Gazaly's tent set a little apart from the encircled Big Top. It was bright red with yellow fringed flounces outlining the entrance to a large square tent. The banner across the top of the entrance said THE GREAT GAZALY AND HIS VERITABLE VORTEX OF FUTURE FORCES. The front section of the tent was topped by a beautifully shaped rotunda from the apex of which shot what looked like small projectiles shaped like question marks which evaporated into the air a full 20 feet above the ground. These had proved to be a great attraction by themselves. The Great Gazaly kept the secret of how they were produced to himself.

This morning the flaps covering the main entrance were drawn. The man himself was obviously not ready to meet the day. Beatrix knew how to alert him to her arrival as Abigail had told her about it. She took hold of the crank handle and turned it three times clockwise thus announcing her presence. Almost immediately, hands pulled open the curtains, and the Great Gazaly stuck his head out and looked quickly left and right. He then pulled Beatrix by the arm into the tent and snapped the flaps closed behind his back. He looked at Beatrix and said hurriedly in a heavy Italian accent, "Ah Miss Bea, you look ravishing today. What can I do for you?"

"I have brought your new jacket to check that it fits," Beatrix said holding up the jacket for his inspection. It was quite dark inside the tent, the only light coming from a magnificent gas-lit chandelier. This was enough, however, for Beatrix to observe his face and notice that he was having trouble meeting her eyes. She continued when he didn't answer her. "I also wanted to thank you for telling my fortune last week, particularly the part about the fact that my parents are most probably alive and still in Australia."

"What? What did you say?" he asked, his focus

suddenly right onto her. "I don't remember that. You must be mistaken."

"But I clearly remember it that way," protested Beatrix.

"No, no, no! You mustn't go around saying things like that. I didn't! I believe your parents are dead. Absolutely."

"But…..," Beatrix began, looking closely at him. "…perhaps you are right."

"Yes, yes, you must go now. Thank you for the jacket. I will try it on and let you know if it fits or not." With that he turned around and stuck his head out between the flaps, looked both ways, and grabbing her arm again pushed her through the gap and closed them quickly behind her. She could hear him tying up the flap closure tapes inside the tent.

Beatrix stood looking at the closed flaps. "Well, what was that all about?" she asked herself.

She decided to walk the other way back to Madame

Chong's so doing a complete circuit of the circus. Beatrix looked across the road and glimpsed their friend Mitchell O'Connor talking to a tall man wearing a caped coat and a top hat. She waved at him but he was obviously deep in conversation and did not see her as he did not wave back. The man in the top hat, however, did see her and fixed a steely gaze on her. She felt a shiver pass over her and decided she must find out who he was. Her attention returned to the carnies and looking ahead, she saw people outside their vans and tents, but by the time she got to them they had disappeared. Usually, she would enjoy a chat with most of them as she passed.

Coming towards her from the opposite direction was Stromlo, the steam-powered man. He suddenly shut down, his head retreating into his shoulders, his pistons silent and his smoking stack emitting nothing but a wisp of left-over smoke. He had become a black and shiny lump of steel. Beatrix wondered if something had happened to him or if seeing her had triggered this reaction.

"Don't be silly. Why would he want to snub me? He has always been friendly. Well, as friendly as a robotic man can be."

In the distance, Beatrix could hear Karl Nagy, the four-armed calliope player, practising. He usually played with fabulous abandon – marches, orchestral pieces, jigs and waltzes. Beatrix grimaced when she heard what he was playing now. It sounded as though he was practising for a funeral – dirges, one after the other. "Had someone died?" Beatrix wondered. She hadn't heard about it if someone had.

By the time she arrived at Madame Chong's tent she was convinced something was wrong and she determined to find out what had brought about this change. It was as though 'something wicked' had passed through their camp and it did not bode well for the future.

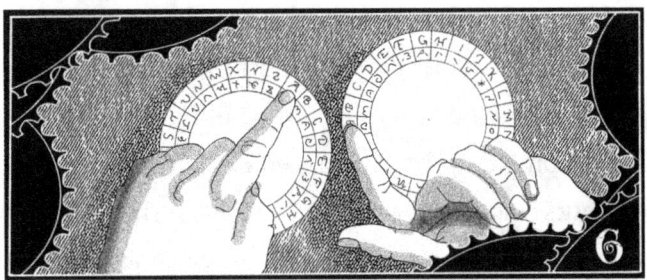

A Meeting

Later that week, Abigail, Beatrix, Zarah, Charlie and Mitchell were gathered together in their tiny van sitting in a tight circle, talking in low tones. The weather had turned from the usual hot days of summer to one where the clouds were gathering and darkening. Humidity was high. Thunder could be heard in the distance. And everyone was uncomfortable.

Beatrix was finishing explaining why she had called them all together for the meeting, "So, by the time I got back from the Great Gazaly's tent, I was convinced that something had happened that very morning which put me right on the outer. And when I got to Madame Chong's it was as if all her pistons had been frozen. She was staring into space and when she saw me she told me to be careful, to be wary of strangers, and never go out alone. I asked her if something had happened and she replied that of course nothing had happened; that she was just warning me to be watchful. The whole conversation was totally out-of-steamwhack."

"I know what you mean," piped up Charlie, "I can't do anything right with Lenny. It started that day I waved at you on your way to the Great Gazaly's." Charlie nodded in agreement. "You're right, Bea, things are totally rustified."

"Well," said Mitchell, "I can tell you ....."

Abigail, not hearing Mitchell, picked up the theme saying, "I have been having similar experiences. Prof Landers no longer wants me to do any performances and the other carnies are avoiding me as if I have some sort of horrible malady. The GG has been a bit nervous since that day. He is, however, keen to continue my apprenticeship and is very pleased with my abilities. He tells me so often. I don't think he can be part of this conspiracy you are all describing."

"Fine, apart from 'the GG'," said Beatrix looking at her older sister with a deep frown, "I think we can safely assume that something has happened that has changed the way the carnies react to us. It must be something significant and we need to find out the way the train-tracks lie. Where will we start? Any ideas?"

"I can tell you what it is if you will let me speak, Miss Beatrix," said Mitchell. Beatrix met his eyes, raised her eyebrows and nodded. "Go ahead," she murmured, her cheeks going a little pink.

"I know for a fact that the circus has been sold to someone powerful in Melbourne. I don't know who it is, but that is what my uncle told me."

"But why," queried Abigail, "would that mean that the carnies no longer want to know us?"

"That's a good question," said Beatrix, her eyes moving to the roof of the caravan as if she could find the answer there, "Madame Chong's attitude had changed when I returned from the Great Gazaly's.

And…," she continued, "she had had a visitor while I was away. I saw him when I was leaving. He wore a bowler hat and a mechanical eye piece."

"Then our first task," Beatrix said slowly, "is to find out the name of the person who has bought the circus. Once we find that out it should lead us to the mysterious visitor who might have been turning the carnies against us."

"Shsh a minute, Beatrix," whispered Zarah, "did you hear that? I think someone is outside listening." She stood up, opened up the door and peeked out into the night. Shaking her head she sat down, "I couldn't see anything. But I was sure I heard something."

"In that case, we should communicate in code so that only we know what it is that we are doing," whispered Beatrix quietly. She looked around to see the others nodding in agreement. "Do you all have your Della Mortic coders? Yes? No? "

She withdrew two small boxes from her pocket. "Right, these are for you, Mitchell and Charlie. There are instructions on how to use the codebreaker and a codemaker as well. Please look after them carefully. We must not let them fall into anyone else's hands. Understand?"

Mitchell and Charlie were looking at their boxes. Charlie's eyes were lit with excitement. "Cogs and gears! This is so pistonomical!"

Mitchell looked at Beatrix from under his hair, his eyes dark and serious. "This is dangerous then, Miss Beatrix?"

"I believe so," responded Beatrix. "Every one of us needs to be very, very careful."

She looked around slowly at her sisters and friends. "Then let's go and find out what is going on."

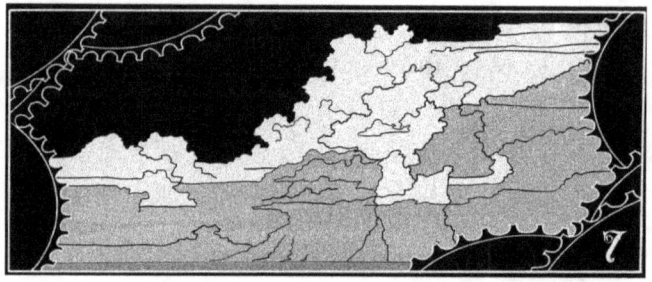

A Synergy Of Sleuths

The following day the pending storm broke and the skies opened. The rain was intense and the thunder and lightning explosive. In its own way, it was a relief, although it kept the sleuths indoors and the public away from the circus. The Ringmaster cancelled three performances, which gave Mitchell and Charlie time to become familiar with their new codemakers. Mitchell stayed home at his uncle's and Charlie studied in the sisters' van.

Over the next few days, the friends quietly went about observing their fellow carnies. The storm had had another consequence. It seemed to have broken the tension a little between the carnies and the sleuths.

****

Lenny had gathered his mini acrobat troupe together the day after the meeting. Lenny looked very worried and the young acrobats looked at each other to see if anyone knew what was up. Charlie whispered into Tiny's, the smallest acrobat's, ear who was sitting next to him, "Any ideas?" Tiny just shrugged his shoulders.

"Troupe!" said Lenny loudly. "Listen up! I have an announcement to make."

The troupe began whispering amongst themselves.

Raising and lowering his hands to quieten the noise Lenny continued, "I am leaving circus at the end of the week and you will have a new leader and teacher from then on."

More whispers and murmurs rose from the troupe.

"I know this will come as a surprise but rest assured that you will still have your place in the troupe even though I am no longer here to look after you. In fact, I can tell you that Mr Flanagan has come here today to meet you. Come forward, Mr Flanagan and meet my, I mean your, troupe of mini acrobats."

A stooped figure wearing a long coat and a felt hat that fell across his face shuffled forward and looked at the children. This man stood in stark contrast to Lenny who was upright, fit and smartly dressed in his shorts and singlet and who usually moved at a smart jogging pace. This man looked unfit and badly dressed. His coat dragged on the ground and barely covered his very round stomach across which lay a chain stretched to breaking point.

"Well, well ..." began Mr Flanagan, "so these are my charges!

The troupe had gone silent and stared at Mr Flanagan with something akin to alarm.

"I'm sure we will get on famously if you behave yourselves and do what you're told. There will definitely be some changes around here and many exciting new skills to learn. Many new skills," Mr Flanagan purred, his steely eyes not reflecting the sweetness of his voice.

Charlie felt Mr Flanagan's eyes upon him and shivered. He looked at Tiny, "I don't like him one bit."

****

Mitchell, apart from when he was running away from his uncle, spent most of his off-duty hours at the circus. He made it his business to approach as many of the carnies as he could trying to find out the name of the man who had bought the circus. He had had little success. Many of the carnies avoided him and, interestingly, those he did meet were not forthcoming about the sale but did sometimes suggest he stay away from the Della Morte sisters. When he queried this, he was met by blank stares or assurances that it would be to his benefit.

This shocked Mitchell and he resolved to alert the sisters as quickly as possible as it seemed that they were somehow of interest to the purchaser. He would send a coded message to Beatrix that very day to warn them.

He had not seen the sisters that day so when he arrived home at his uncle's he went to his room to compose the message to Beatrix. Before he was able to do this, however, his uncle cornered him as he made his way from the back door to his room.

"Have you been at the circus today, Mitch my boyo?" Uncle Patrick asked him.

"Yes, sir. Is something wrong?" responded Mitchell.

"No, well, yes in a way there is. I don't like your running after those sisters all the time. I think you should stay away from the circus for a while, at least until ……." His uncle's voice trailed off.

"Until what?"

"Oh, nothing. Just stay here, I have work for you to do and I need you here. Also, I must say that those sisters are not for you. So here you will stay and do your work where you cannot be forever meeting up with them. My two girls will ensure that that happens. Won't you girls?" Uncle Patrick pointed at his two navvies who had accompanied Patrick on this errand of his, their goggles glinting in the morning light which filled the room through the high windows.

Trudie was small, wiry and muscular with an abundance of blonde curls that often misled people who did not know her into thinking she was weak and easily overcome. Far from it; she was a fierce little terrier who learned her craft in the boxing rings of the slums of Dublin before emigrating to Melbourne in 1875 after she had lost her left eye to a particularly vicious left hook. She now sported a blue glass eye which she sometimes removed for a party trick. She wore trousers, boots, white shirt and black vest. When her eye socket needed a rest, she covered it with a black eye patch.

In contrast, Rosalie was a giant of a woman, at least six feet tall and well-built as they say. Her pants were tight and her boots sprouted gleaming silver spurs. She had fled Texas during the American Civil War and loved what was becoming known as the American Cowboy look. A Stetson hat sat firmly on her head and her jacket was tight fitting and nipped in severely at the waist. She tipped her hat at her boss to show agreement with his directions to keep his nephew confined to the premises.

Mitchell was intrigued. He continued to question his uncle but he found himself talking to Patrick's back as he walked away. His uncle was generally not interested in how Mitchell spent his spare time and sent his enforcers after him only if he stayed out all night. He was free to come and go as he pleased outside of his working hours. Trudie and Rosalie would be watching him from now on and going to the circus would not be an option.

Mitchell watched as his uncle disappeared. "Things are moving faster than a train with an open throttle," he said to himself. "I'd better hurry up." He opened the door to his room and closed it quickly behind him. He withdrew his code-maker and rule book from their box under his bed and sat at a small table under the window that looked onto the lane which ran behind his uncle's establishment. He lit a kerosene lamp with his flint matchbox and withdrew a piece of paper and his pencil from the drawer. First, he wrote out his message in English and signed it "Your friend, Mitchell." He smiled at this and had a small chuckle to himself.

He placed his codemaker down on the desk and

opened his rule book. He first decided on the key he would use and wrote it down in sequence at the top right of the message. This was SCCL4. He set his codemaker circles as required by this and started reading off the code letter by letter until he had completed his message.

The message read:

ϕ𝜦 𝜐𝜐𝜐 ⁄ℨ𝜦'+𝜦𝜦 m 𝜦 𝜦𝜦ℨ⁰
𝜦𝜦𝜦' ⁰𝜦 𝜐𝜐+ℽ𝜦ℨ𝜦 Γ✳ ⁰Γℽ𝜐𝜐
+𝜦𝜦+ ⌒ℱℽ 𝜦Γ⁰ ⌒ℱℽ𝜦 𝜐𝜦 𝜐𝜐+⁰𝜦𝜐𝜐
𝜦𝜦⁰ 𝜦Γ ⁰𝜦𝜦Γ✳⁰𝜦 ⁄ℨ⁰ ⁰m+𝜦𝜦
𝜦𝜦𝜦𝜐ℽ⁊ ʊ𝜦ℱϕ Γℱ⌒ ℱΓ
⌒ℱℽ𝜦 ʊ𝜦𝜦Γ⁰
ϕ𝜦 +𝜦𝜦⁊⁊

He folded the message and the code settings ready for posting and wrote on the front:

> Miss Beatrix Della Morte
>
> C/- Madam Chong
>
> The Antipodean Circus of Oddities and
>
> Amazing Sights
>
> Cnr Bourke and Spring Streets
>
> MELBOURNE

Now he had to decide how to get the message to Beatrix in the shortest possible time. Under the new rules he knew he was being watched and would be physically prevented from leaving home. So, what to do?

The lane outside his window was often used as a shortcut through the city. It was also a shortcut to the circus grounds. He looked through his window hoping to see someone to whom he could give the letter to take to Beatrix. After some time he saw Gregorio, one of the Clownspringers loping leisurely along the street. He knew Gregorio quite well as Gregorio had been teaching Mitchell the secrets of springing. Mitchell knocked on his window as Gregorio came near. Gregorio slowed and stopped outside leaning on the wall beside the window for support. Mitchell opened the window and holding out the message he asked, "Great scuttlebuts! Gregorio? Fancy seeing you here. Are you on your way to the circus?"

"I am that, Mr. Mitchell." replied Gregorio. "What can I do for you?"

"Would you do me a favour and take this letter to Miss Beatrix? She works with Madam Chong or could you take it directly to her caravan. I'll pay you to do it."

Gregorio took the letter and a coin offered by Mitchell and tucked it inside his jacket, nodding. "That I can do. Goodbye for now."

Gregorio started springing down the street, with just a glance behind to wave at Mitchell who was leaning out of the window.

Beatrix and Abigail were sitting in their caravan the next night when Zarah and Charlie came home. The girls could hear them in deep conversation outside the door about something. Eventually the younger ones came into the caravan obviously with something to say.

"Charlie needs to pass onto to you what has been happening in the troupe," began Zarah.

Charlie nodded in agreement saying, "I've checked outside and no-one is out there listening to us.

Charlie continued "You know that Lenny has left the circus, Well, we think that there is something cogdodgy about that new Mr Flanagan. He has selected a few members of the troupe for what he calls 'Advanced Training'. He tells the rest of us to keep practising our routines and takes the chosen ones off to the field over there behind the large oak tree. I have followed them and I think that he is teaching them to pick pockets."

"Oh, no! Surely not!" exclaimed Abigail, shocked at the very thought of it.

"Oh, yes!" said Charlie. "He has them operating in pairs; one distracts the victim (who is played by Mr. Flanagan) and one reaches into his pocket and lifts whatever is in there, trying to do so in complete secrecy.

"And if Mr. Flanagan feels his pocket being picked, he slaps the sloppy pickpocket across the head," Charlie added.

Beatrix looked at Charlie and said, "You should

make sure you are not selected for advanced training. There are some skills you do not need."

Charlie looked at Zarah and then lowered his eyes. "Of course not," murmured Charlie, his hands disappearing behind his back, "I would never do something like that." There was really no need for the others to know he had been going to advanced training for three days now.

****

Abigail and Professor Landers were sitting in his tent both practising their memory routines. The rain was now long forgotten and the dry hot wind of the Melbourne summer was blowing through the tent from the north. The mud had dried outside and the wind was causing bursts of dust to enter the tent. Abigail stood up and closed the flaps to keep the dust out.

"That's better, don't you think, Professor Landers?" she asked.

Professor Landers murmured, "Yes, it is, thank you."

"Professor, I have been meaning to ask you about a rumour I've heard around the circus."

"Mmmmm?"

"Is it true that the circus has been sold to a powerful Melbourne man? Do you know who he is?"

The Professor lowered his eyeglasses and look up at Abigail who was still standing near the tent flaps.

"I have heard the rumour. I have also heard that he is a dangerous man."

"Really? Is there any connection between that man and the reason you won't allow me to perform in the Big Top anymore?"

Professor Landers did not respond to this question. He put his glasses back on and returned to his practice. The conversation was at an end.

****

By the end of the week the sisters and Charlie had heard nothing concrete about the identities of the purchaser or the man in the bowler hat and mechanical eyepiece. They had heard about the introduction of changes and new staff into the circus and vague feelings of unease had been conveyed to them. They really had learned very little.

"Well," said Beatrix, "that was a week of futile activity. And has anyone seen Mitchell? I haven't heard a word from him. Anyone? I admit that I am a little worried about him. It's not like him at all."

Abigail shook her head saying, "Why don't we give him another day. It's Saturday tomorrow and he might come then. When he arrives, we'll gather out of doors under the jacaranda tree where we will be sure we cannot be overhead and decide what to do next. What do you think?"

"That at least sounds like a plan," murmured Zarah, who was impatient to be getting on with the investigation.

"So, it's agreed then. Let's say 10 o'clock under the jacaranda tree," said Beatrix calling the meeting to a close.

Abduction By Moonlight

The sisters and Charlie had settled down to sleep that night. A cool breeze drifted in from outside and the interior of the van was lit softly by moonlight coming in through the windows.

Zarah had been suffering from the heat and early in the summer she had rigged up a long piece of canvas along the centre of the ceiling which could be moved like a giant fan to move the air in the van. If it was extremely hot she would take down the canvas and soak it in water before rehanging it. The fan could be operated by any of the inmates of the van simply by pulling on a rope tied to the canvas. Sometimes Zarah tied the fan to her ankle so that the fan moved whenever she turned over.

That night, however, the canvas was hanging freely and moving gently in the breeze. All that could be heard, had the roommates been awake, was the sound of the moving canvas and the usual variety of night sounds of a city like Melbourne. That is, until in the distance came the unmistakable trumpet of one of the circus's steam-powered elephants. It woke Zarah and she lay in her bed listening to the breathing of her fellow van occupants but she was not sure what had awakened her so she turned over and went back to sleep.

****

Outside, avoiding patches of moonlight, three dark figures slunk their way across the open spaces until they reached the small caravan alongside the Ringmaster's van. The door and windows on the van could be locked both from the inside and the outside, it once having been used to keep disorderly carnies safe for the night and everyone else safe from them.

The three figures quietly locked the door and windows from the outside, kicked away the chocks which stopped the caravan from rolling and assembled at the end of the van where the A-frame was located which was usually hitched to another van or a steam engine for transportation. In unison, they lifted the A-frame and heaving, rocked the van to and fro until it started to move.

****

Charlie had been dreaming about his favourite activity, which was pushing buttons. This was how he had received his name, Charlie Buttons. As soon as he had learned to walk he would push every button he could find. He had been fearless in doing this and had been the unknowing cause of some very nasty incidents, like the time he pushed the red button on the cable car which stopped so abruptly that the cable underneath had broken. He had been labelled incorrigible and had ended up at the age of eleven in the Melbourne Boys' Asylum in South Melbourne. He had just dreamed he had pushed a bright green button which had started up an enormous swinging pendulum when he felt he really was swinging through the air. Well, he was not swinging, but the caravan in which he slept was swinging and then began to move smoothly. Charlie shook his head, trying to make sense of what was happening.

He jumped out of bed and ran to the door. In vain he tried to open it.

"Wake up, everyone!" he whispered. "We are being moved, holus-bolus. Van and all!"

The others woke up and soon picked up on the strangeness of what was happening. Beatrix smothered a shriek and jumped out of bed, her hands to her mouth. Abigail stood on her bed trying to unlock the window closest to her. Zarah was up and checking all the locks.

"It seems to me that we are locked in here and are being abducted by a person or persons unknown," said Zarah trying to keep the excitement out of her voice. She was sensitive to the fact that her older sisters did not share her love of adventure and often had to tone down her enjoyment of the unexpected and bizarre.

"Shush now," Zarah held up her finger to her mouth. "We don't want whoever is stealing us away to know we are awake before we can think of a way to escape. Let me think."

Zarah started carefully checking all the walls and the ceiling looking for weaknesses in the fabric of the van but found nothing. She looked down at her feet and pushed with one foot feeling the giving nature of floorboards. She began to crawl under the bunks and table investigating the floor of the van by feeling with her hands. They could not risk lighting a lamp which would alert their abductors to the fact that they were awake. Suddenly a hand emerged from under one of the beds accompanied by a whispered, "Hand me my arm brace."

Charlie quickly retrieved Zarah's arm brace which contained her favourite tools and pushed it into the waiting hand. After some soft scratching sounds a floorboard appeared, to be taken by Charlie and placed on the table. This was followed by another and another. Last to appear was Zarah who slivered out from under the bed holding a screwdriver in one hand and her arm brace in the other.

"That should do it," she said softly. The others looked at her for an explanation. But she shook her head. There would be time for talking afterwards.

Now they needed to act.

"Abigail," said Zarah. "Where are we?"

"We are about halfway between the Big Top and the Entourage Shed. I can see the doors are open and one of the elephants appears to be moving out of the shed."

"It seems that their plan is to take us away from circus using the elephant. We could," Zarah said consideringly, "wait for them to deliver us to whoever wants us captured ...."

"No! No!" squealed Beatrix through her hands.

".... which would then show us who is behind all this," Zarah continued. "Or we could escape now while we have time."

"Wait?" Only Zarah showed her hand.

"Or, escape now?" Three other hands could be seen in the moonlight.

"Sockologer! Let's do it then! Let Operation Vanish begin!" Zarah was really enjoying this. "I will drop to the ground through the hole I have made in the floor of the van, lay on the ground and then come up once the van has passed over me and unlock the door at the back. Then you can all escape through the open back door. Easy Steamy!"

"I'm scared. What if they catch us?" whispered Beatrix through her hands which still covering her mouth.

"It would appear, Beatrix, that we are already caught," said Abigail. "But I know what you mean."

"Then," replied Zarah as she bent down to start the operation, "we run like the wind until we lose them and meet up at the place under the seats in the big top where we spent our first night."

Meanwhile, the three abductors were beginning to tire as the surface over which they were pulling the van was rough and potholed. However, whatever incentive had been placed before them was sufficient for them to continue toiling. A couple of them were starting to breathe heavily, but the one at the head of the A-frame was doing his part in pulling the van with ease.

Zarah was slowly lowering herself into position prior to allowing herself to fall to the ground. Just as she felt the ground under her feet, one of the van wheels dropped into a pothole and Zarah let out a small "Oh!" of surprise as she dropped to the ground.

The van immediately stopped moving and the abductor on the side closest to where Zarah now lay hissed, "What was that? Did you hear that?"

The leader looked over his shoulder, "Yes I did hear something. Check that all the windows and the door are secured. We are almost there, so hustle up."

Zarah froze under the van and then rolled as quietly as she could to the darkest part close to a wheel and away from the moonlit parts of the ground. She coiled herself into as tiny a package as she could and kept as still as possible.

From her viewpoint she could see two legs and two

feet shod in the boots the clowns wore and to which they attached their springers. "So," she thought, "at least one of these three thugs is a Clownspringer!" The legs walked around the edge of the van reaching up on tip toes to check the fastenings of the windows and the door. The legs moved to the front of the van and Zarah breathed out in relief and relaxed a little.

"Did you check under the van?" croaked the voice of the leader trying to keep his voice down as low as possible.

Zarah stopped breathing again and heard rather saw the same legs walk to the side of the van where she was hiding. He must have leaned down because Zarah could almost feel his breath as he scanned under the van. Nothing happened for a full minute until Zarah saw a hand waving around under the van floor. It almost hit her but she managed to sway out of reach. The hand withdrew and after a few seconds she heard the legs moving towards the front of the van.

"Nothing," the Clownspringer reported.

At that the three abductors started to heave again to get the van started. This gave Zarah time to roll into the centre of the space where she would be safest. The van started to move and once it had moved off from over the top of Zarah she jumped up and ran quickly to the back of the van and unfastened the lock on the door. It opened from the inside and the remaining three jumped as quietly as they could to the ground.

Before they had time to run for it, the van stopped. The sudden lightening of the van had alerted the abductors that something had happened and the leader ran to the side of the van and hissed to his comrades.

"They've escaped. After them or we'll be for it!"

At this the young people took off in all directions running as fast as they could. They ran as if their lives depended on it and as far as they knew, this was the case.

Regrouping

Abigail huddled into a corner in that part of the Big Top where she and her sisters and friends had spent their first night at the circus under the seats. She concentrated on her breathing trying to bring it under control. This calmed her down and her senses became aware of the sounds outside the tent. She could hear running feet, some light and some heavy. She could hear grunts and soft shouts. She knew the race was on.

As there had been three abductors and four escapees one of the young people had had an easy time of it. That had been Abigail. However, she had not known that as she ran until she looked over her shoulder and had seen that she was not being chased. She slowed down to a fast walk and gasped at what she saw parked at the aeroport behind the circus grounds. She picked up her speed and made straight for the Big Top and felt her way to the agreed meeting place.

That had been ten minutes ago and now she was waiting anxiously for the others to join her. Her lively imagination had them all captured and returned to the caravan for delivery to whoever was giving the orders. Then they would come looking for her!

She jumped at every small sound and tried to make herself as small as she could. She deliberately slowed her breathing and tried to make it as silent as possible. She sat and waited and pondered on what she had seen and what it meant.

Her ears pricked up when she heard a rustle near the entrance to the tent. She froze and held her breath. This could be an abductor who was looking for her! She peered into the darkness but could see nothing. Her heartbeat increased and she struggled to keep her hands from shaking. She was unable to keep herself from uttering a small groan.

At this the rustling stopped and she heard a very

feminine voice call softly, "Who is that? Is that you Abigail?"

"Beatrix? Is that you? Yes, it's me," whispered Abigail with a very relieved sigh. "Oh, Giovanni! Thank goodness!"

The rustling restarted and Abigail felt a hand on her shoulder and Beatrix whispering in her ear. "The others still not here, then?"

Abigail shook her head and the two settled as close as possible to each other to wait.

They had to wait another hour for Zarah and Charlie to turn up. These two finally crept into the space and sat down on the side of Abigail opposite to where Beatrix was leaning. Abigail decided to remain silent on what she had seen. The other three had had enough excitement for one night. They would wait for sunrise before they would venture outside.

Emergence

Abigail had not slept at all. She kept watch over the younger ones until the first rays of the sun started to seep through the gaps in the tent canvas. She then gently woke them up and they moved to the front flaps of the tent's entrance. Zarah had been peering through the gap between the flaps when she suddenly withdrew her head and gasped, "Well, I never! You won't believe what I can see?"

"What is it? What can you see?" Beatrix wanted to know, her confidence growing along with the sunlight.

Zarah drew aside one of the flaps so the others could see outside. "See for yourselves," she said with a flourish of her free hand. Cautiously, the others moved toward the open flap and looked outside.

It was early morning so not many carnies were awake and moving about yet. As they scanned the scene, one by one they made out what Zarah had found so surprising. Sitting right where it had for several weeks was their very own caravan, sitting there as if nothing had happened during the night, sitting there in all its usual lack of repair and maintenance. Zarah pointed over to the Entourage Shed where the doors were closed, portraying an innocence that the friends knew from recent experience was false.

The cook was opening the victualling van getting ready to feed the early risers. Abigail pointed to it saying, "Let's prepare for today. I think we should start with breakfast as there are plenty of people about. We need to keep to our routines and act as if nothing happened. We'll meet at 10 o'clock just as planned under the jacaranda tree. I think we must move quickly now, and remember everyone, be careful out there."

Strategies

That day was just like the rest of that week. Melbourne had endured five continuous days over 100 degrees Fahrenheit and Saturday was looking to be just as hot. Melbournians were used to these heatwaves. However, the Della Morte sisters were suffering. England had a much milder summer climate, rarely if ever reaching these temperatures. Two of these English roses were wilting.

The jacaranda tree provided some shade but by 10 o'clock in the morning the sun was scorching down from a cloudless sky. Charlie had adopted shorts and singlet as was the wont of the mini acrobat troupe. Zarah didn't feel the heat except at night. Beatrix had discarded her jacket and was dressed in blouse and skirt with sandals on her feet. Abigail had adapted the least well to the climate and was wearing her blouse, long skirt and boots. She was accustomed to wear clothes expected of a young lady in England and found it hard to break away from these even if it meant she was uncomfortable. She wore a straw hat and carried a fan always. She was leaning heavily against the trunk of the tree waving the fan vigorously.

"Mitchell would usually be here by now. I think we should start without him," Abigail said wearily. "I can't wait to get out of this heat."

"Well," piped up Zarah, "If you didn't wear so many clothes you wouldn't be so hot."

"Just trying to be helpful," continued Zarah in answer to Abigail's stare at what she took to be her little sister's disrespectful attitude.

"She's right, you know. I could run you up lighter clothes if you like," added Beatrix.

Abigail in a rush to get out of the heat ignored all

the talk of clothes and said, "Right then. What do we know? We know that:

- The circus has been bought by a powerful Melbourne man.
- We don't know who he is.
- Some, if not all, of the carnies won't or are afraid to associate with us.
- There are changes happening quickly in the circus which could be seen as somewhat on the criminal side such as pick-pocketing training and abduction.
- Someone is very interested in capturing the four of us for reasons unknown, and,
- Mitchell is missing from the circus."

Zarah immediately put up her hand. She was a well brought up young girl, no matter what Abigail's current opinion of her was. "I saw the boots of the thug who searched the van after I dropped out through the floor," said Zarah. "They were the boots of a Clownspringer, so at least one of those was in on it."

Beatrix nodded. "The leader was incredibly strong

and was most probably Brutus the Strongman." She paused, then, "I am worried about Mitchell. I am going into town to visit his uncle's place of business and find out why he has stopped coming to the circus," said Beatrix softly. "I hope he hasn't stopped liking me, I mean us." Zarah and Abigail both raised their eyebrows and exchanged knowing glances.

The group sat in silence for a few minutes.

"I have something to tell you about what I saw last night," began Abigail. The rest of the group looked at her curiously. Abigail hesitated before continuing, "I saw the front end of a zeppelin poking out from where it was moored behind the Big Top."

Zarah started to protest, "So what! There are plenty of zeppelins around Melb…….."

Abigail held up her hand and stopped her before whispering, "You don't understand. This was *The Zeppelin*, the one that scooped up Mother and Father. I recognised it by the front of the craft. It stood open, just as it had when we saw it the night of the storm, when it swallowed our parents."

"What was it doing there?" Zarah asked. Abigail's face started to wrinkle up as if she were trying to make a decision; so much so that Beatrix finally said, "Abigail, what is the matter with you? You look like you have swallowed a handful of iron filings. Come on, spill them out, what do you think it was doing there?"

Abigail once again fell into a whisper, "I think it was waiting there for a special delivery.

"I think it was waiting there to take delivery of our caravan, with us in it.

"Whoever has our parents now knows where we are and wants to capture us also. We need to identify this person and he will, I believe, lead us to mother and father."

Beatrix, Zarah and Charlie were silent at this. What had at first been an adventure at the circus was now a very dangerous situation, indeed. They had all been so caught up in the mystery of the circus turning against them they had almost forgotten that their first goal had been to find their parents.

Abigail closed her eyes and said, "I am also worried, about the GG. He has changed since that day that you, Beatrix, delivered his new jacket. Prior to that he would share all the algorithms with me, but lately he has started to do his own, in secret, and then call for Tiny, one of the mini acrobats, and give him an envelope to take somewhere. It can't be far as Tiny is usually back within 30 minutes."

Abigail's enthusiasm for the chase was picking up as if her loyalty to the GG had been stretched too far and she was ready to include him in their search for what lay behind their falling out of favour. "I would really like to know where Tiny takes the Great Gazaly's envelopes. Charlie, could you take on this task? Follow Tiny and try not to be seen. Report back to us as soon as possible," instructed Abigail.

"Beatrix, you are going to visit Mitchell. His non-appearance is a worry for all of us, but especially for you it seems," said Abigail with a kind smile to her sister. "Do you want to take Zarah with you?"

"No, no," interposed Zarah. "I have something else I want to investigate, but I can't tell you about it until I am sure. And anyway, Beatrix doesn't want me tagging along when she goes to visit Mitchell."

Abigail had really taken over the meeting and she now closed it with a warning, "Please all be careful and don't put yourselves into dangerous situations. I too have something to do. I believe that the GG knows more than he is saying and I intend to question him closely and attempt to find out what it is. Off you go and get busy sleuthing. We must identify the owner of the zeppelin. I am sure that he is the key to all that has been happening here at the circus and is heavily involved in the abduction of our parents."

A Safe Conundrum

Zarah was the first to leave the shade of the jacaranda tree and began an unhurried walk around the outside of the Big Top. She didn't want to call attention to where she was going and by way of diverting suspicions, stopped to talk to any of the carnies who would speak to her. When she got to the Ringmaster's van she sauntered past it and then took up a position a little away and started to play with the rubber ball that she extracted from her pocket, mostly just bouncing and catching it. There was only a short time until lunch and she knew that the Ringmaster liked to eat with the other carnies. Eventually, the Ringmaster emerged from his van, closing his door behind and took off at a steady pace towards the victualling area.

Zarah waited five minutes, then wandered up to the door of the Ringmaster's van and knocked. She looked around swiftly, checking that no-one was watching, before slipping quietly through the door. She had been in this van once before and had noticed what she believed would be a good place to keep something away from curious eyes. It was quite dark in the van, as the Ringmaster had closed his curtains, and Zarah kept very still while she allowed her eyes to adjust after the bright sun outside.

The van had two rooms – an office where the Ringmaster undertook his business and another room hidden behind a curtain to the rear. Zarah moved quietly to the curtain and pulled it aside. As she had suspected this was the bedroom with a bedside table, cupboard for clothes and in the corner, a large black iron safe. Zarah slid to her knees in front of the safe and tried to turn the wheel. Zarah was a skillful lock picker. She even had her own set of tools that she carried with her always. Before she retrieved her tools, however, she let out a low whistle. "Well, look at this now. I've never seen one of these in the flesh." To the left of the wheel, was a round dial with numbers encircling it. Zarah understood the theory behind the dial but had not had the opportunity to attempt to open one. Her face broke into a wide smile and she rubbed her hands together with what can only be called excited anticipation. She looked around her and not seeing what she needed moved around the curtain and into the office. She heard the sound of footsteps outside and had just enough time to sit down on the visitor's chair when the door opened and the Ringmaster entered. He stopped abruptly when he saw there was someone in his van.

"What in the name of all that's steamy are you doing here?" he asked, obviously annoyed to find her there. "You're one of the sisters, aren't you?"

"I was waiting for you, sir," said Zarah, giving him a small smile. "There was something I wanted to ask you," she added shyly.

"Well, hurry up then. I've never been so hungry. What is it?" the Ringmaster grumbled as he looked around him for whatever it was that had drawn him back to his van. Ah, there it is," he said as he picked up a notebook that had been lying on the desk.

"Well?" he demanded, tapping his foot, wanting to be off.

"Well, I've been working on polishing the elephants for a few weeks now and was hoping for a chance to do some real engineering work and ....."

"That's enough!" interrupted the Ringmaster. "You work for the Chief Engineer. You must ask her. I can't help you. Be off now!"

He held the door open and Zarah passed through. He followed closely behind, locking the door behind him. Zarah noticed this but she smirked, comfortable in her lock-picking prowess. He couldn't keep her out if she wanted to get in.

"I'll try another day. I need something first anyway," Zarah promised herself as she sauntered away.

Beatrix Visits Uncle Patrick's Establishment

Beatrix knew that a cable car ran along Swanston Street north to the Market Square in North Melbourne, but as she didn't have any money at all, she would need to walk there. She also knew that she was worried about Mitchell, who for all his annoying ways, had been a good and steadfast friend to her and her sisters. She told herself that he was nothing special to her and that she would do the

same for Charlie Buttons but she also felt a sense of comradeship with Mitchell she didn't feel for Charlie. She had to admit that she had a soft spot for him. At home in England, she would not have given him a second glance. She was of the privileged classes and he was an Irish peasant class boy. But out here in Australia those differences seemed less important than a sense of humour and a liking for well-designed clothes in common. She just had to make sure that he was alright.

Once she arrived at the square she stopped and looked around with wonder. The square was lined with many exciting and colourful establishments such as the toyseller's, the clock shop and the alchemy factory and store. People were milling about, crisscrossing the square, going about their business, oblivious it seemed to Beatrix to the huge contraption in the centre of the square – the Carousel of Shame.

The Carousel of Shame was an enormous rotating contraption which was driven by a medium-sized steam engine which worked the gears, shafts and pulleys that turned three levels of cages. Inside the cages crouched or sat individuals who definitely were not enjoying the experience. The noise associated with the rotation of the carousel was grating and offensive. However, the greatest noise was generated by the yelling and screaming exchanges between the public and the people in the cages. Time in the carousel was handed out to people deemed to have broken the rules of the society. These rules included requirements to be innovative, polite and well presented. Any one of the citizens could be picked up by jet-packed flying members of the constabulary, the Floppers. These floppers didn't wait for trials as these were considered unnecessary for petty crimes.

Beatrix heard before she saw the rotten tomatoes hitting the sides of the cages. Many members of the public considered throwing bad food at the inmates as great sport. Some enterprising young boys and girls made a living of sorts selling rotting food for just this purpose. Beatrix scrunched up her nose, placed her hands over her ears and with her head firmly averted from the carousel made her way quickly to the side of the square and to Mitchell's uncle's business.

Mitchell's Uncle Patrick had a thriving enterprise in the patent business. He marketed himself as enabling budding inventors to obtain the patents for their inventions. Sometimes he went so far as to go through the process required on behalf of the inventor. This was of course in return for a share of the patent itself. This could be up to 80% for Uncle Patrick and 20% for the inventor, depending on the naiveté of the inventor. Of course, this fact was not part of Uncle Patrick's marketing strategy. Uncle Patrick employed Trudie and Rosalie as 'specialist enablers' to encourage good outcomes of negotiations.

In addition, Uncle Patrick ran a small printing business which was the more public face of the O'Connor printing and patent businesses. Beatrix had not met Uncle Patrick before and was a little nervous of doing so. She was well aware that he discouraged Mitchell from being friends with the Della Morte sisters for reasons that she did not understand.

As she was standing looking at the door of the establishment, it opened and a tall man in a caped coat and top hat exited and walked towards the carousel, stopping to purchase some rotten tomatoes.

He picked his victim, a thief in ragged clothes, and threw his tomatoes at this poor unfortunate, all of them meeting their target with plenty of red liquid now staining his face and clothes. Beatrix screwed her nose up and glared at the back of the man as he left the square.

But she was on a mission, so she resolutely walked to the door and pushed it open and entered the shop front. A steam-powered customer-alerting device was sitting on the desk. She pulled the lever attached and a short tune played with a range of alarming notes. She waited but nothing happened. She pulled the lever once more and still nothing happened. On her third try a pair of doors opened behind the desk and a man of medium height with sandy hair moved through the doors and closed them behind him. He had piercing blue eyes which he turned towards Beatrix. Beatrix was unnerved by his stare but managed to stammer that she would like to speak to Mitchell if that were possible, please. "My nephew is working at this time and cannot be disturbed," Patrick O'Connor barked at Beatrix and quickly opened the doors and left the room with a sharp snapping shut of the doors behind him.

Beatrix was stunned and returned to the street. She noticed a narrow lane leading down the side of the building. She looked around her and quietly made her way into the lane. When she reached the end of the lane she turned left. There were windows across the back of the building and what must be the back door. She tried the handle, but found it locked. She was peering through one of the windows when she spied Mitchell working at a desk facing the window. His blond head was bent forward and he was writing. Beatrix watched him for a moment feeling a fondness for that head that surprised her. She knocked softly on the window and Mitchell raised his head. He shaded his eyes and blinked. At this Beatrix backed off allowing Mitchell to see her face. Smiling he bent forward to open the sash window and beckon her forward.

"Miss Beatrix," he whispered urgently. "What are you doing here?" As he said this he looked quickly behind him and up and down the street through the window.

"I've come to see if you are alright. We haven't seen

you or heard from you for days and we were worried about you," Beatrix said hurriedly in a whisper.

Mitchell opened his eyes wide. "I'm fine, confined and not allowed to leave. Didn't you get my note?"

"What note?"

"The note I sent to you with Gregorio, several days ago," Mitchell said slowly thinking about the day he had been warned off the sisters by his uncle and had sent the encoded message to Beatrix. He continued, "The note that warned that you were in danger and needed to be extra careful."

"Well, that might have come in handy, because last night some thugs tried to abduct us," Beatrix whispered urgently, "and we think that whoever kidnapped our parents is now after us!"

The Antipodean Circus of Oddities and Amazing Sights

Melbourne 1889

A Small Invention

Zarah had almost finished for the afternoon; the elephants were ready for the evening performance clean and shining. She descended her elephant by sliding down the trunk and jumping lightly onto the ground.

"Be seeing you tonight, Oily," she called as she made her way to the side exit door. Oily waved as he left for the day. Just before she reached the door, however, she looked quickly around and seeing no-one slipped quietly into the engineering area where she stood listening. She started when she saw the Chief Engineer staring at her fixedly from behind a large engine which she must have been repairing.

"You want something, stowaway, or are you just

casing the joint?" the Chief Engineer demanded.

"Well," began Zarah looking furiously for a good reason for being there and then decided that the truth would do. "I was hoping to maybe find some scraps of metal and rubber and try to build something using some of the tools."

"What sort of something?"

"I don't know. It depends on what I find lying around that isn't needed or wanted anymore."

"Alright, you have 30 minutes before I close up."

Zarah scurried to the other side of the shed looking for anything useful until she found the perfect scraps for what she had in mind. She picked up two pieces of tin, a piece of string and a small length of rubber hosing. She moved to one of the benches and bent over her treasure banging and nailing. Just before the Chief Engineer shut the shed Zarah looked admiringly at what she had created and scooted through the narrow gap between the closing doors.

Charlie Goes Sleuthing

Charlie Buttons was a very curious boy. He liked nothing better than to discover how something or someone worked. He was fascinated by all kinds of buttons. In particular, he loved the type of buttons that you pushed. To Charlie, push buttons were an invitation, especially if they were coloured red or had the words 'Do Not Push' written beside them. He just couldn't help himself. In his short  life this had led to some unfortunate events, such as when he pushed a particularly enticing looking red button just inside the door to the Melbourne Gold Exchange. Immediately enormous shutters fell down across the entry doors and each of the customer service areas. Bells started ringing; people began screaming; and a tough-looking man in uniform picked up Charlie off the ground by the collar of his shirt. Charlie's legs were in motion trying to run but traversing nothing but thin air. That was the first time Charlie had been sent to the Boy's Asylum. It wasn't, however, the last.

There were no buttons on offer where he was standing outside the Great Gazaly's tent, half hiding behind the van across the way. Abigail had said that Tiny usually called in to see the Great Gazaly about 4.00 pm. Right on time, Tiny sauntered down the avenue of tents and caravans, hands in pockets and whistling a tune his Irish grandfather had taught him, 'The Luck of the Irish'. He stopped outside the Great Gazali's tent and the crank handle to announce his arrival. Almost immediately an arm shot out of the opening and pulled Tiny inside, right in the middle of his favourite part of the tune. The Great Gazaly's head popped outside, checked both ways and disappeared back inside, not seeing Charlie who had pulled back behind the side of the caravan.

Minutes later, the whole scene played out in reverse: the Great Gazaly checking that no one was watching and Tiny being pushed quickly out through the opening in the tent, followed by the Great Gazaly once again checking that his action was unseen. Charlie had started to take off after Tiny but pulled back just in time to avoid being spotted.

Once Charlie was sure he was not being observed, he hurried after Tiny. He could see him ahead running out of the circus down Spring Street towards East Melbourne. Tiny was a good little runner and was dodging and weaving through the crowds that lined the hotel and entertainment district that was Spring Street. Charlie had to use all his strength and speed to keep him in sight. Once Tiny reached Victoria Parade he turned right and jumped across the cable line, narrowly missing a swaying cable car. The driver of the cable car clanged loudly at Tiny and shook his fist at him. Charlie waited until the car had passed before jumping nimbly across the line and following Tiny down the street. Tiny ran swiftly past the hospital on the corner and skidded to a halt outside a property surrounded by a tall stone fence and wooden gate with an iron grille.

Charlie caught Tiny just as he was about to pull the rope hanging beside the gate. Charlie grabbed his arm and squeezed it a little and pulled him around the corner to where they couldn't be seen from the property. Tiny turned towards him and pulled his arm free. He rubbed where Charlie had squeezed and frowning asked, "Hello Charlie, what's up? What are you doing here? Did you follow me?"

"My friends, the Della Morte sisters, are in danger and I think perhaps you are involved," Charlie said staring into Tiny's eyes, which shifted away from Charlie's stare and looked around and behind him.

"I have no idea what you're talkin' about. I wouldn't harm your friends. I think they are just steamtastic," returned Tiny, wide eyed.

Charlie considered this and said, "Perhaps you don't' know exactly what's going on but we know that you frequently pick up something from the Great Gazaly and it looks to me that you deliver it here to this address. We need to know what that is."

Tiny started whining, "I don't know nuthin'. I run errands, that's all. That's all."

"All right, all right! Show me what you are delivering today and I will teach you that acrobatic trick you are having trouble with," Charlie conceded.

Tiny withdrew a white piece of paper from his pocket and held it out to Charlie.

Charlie laughed at what he saw. The paper had been folded over several times and was wrapped with a fine piece of paper cut from, but still attached to the paper. Carefully, using a slim tool he pulled from his pocket he levered away the wrapping and opened the letter. Charlie's abilities at reading were rudimentary but he could make out what was written there. He pulled a piece of paper and a pencil out of his capacious pocket and copied down the contents of the letter. Again, carefully, he refolded the paper and replaced the wrapping sliver as before. Nobody would know the letter had been opened. Breaking letter locks and relocking them without detection was quite a skill and Charlie smiled to himself.

"Right, now you tell me what happens before you pick up the letter from the Great Gazaly and I'll let you go," Charlie said as he leaned over Tiny and returned the letter.

"The Ringmaster has me summoned to his office. He hands over the letter to me. I take it to the Great Gazaly. The Great Gazaly goes behind his curtain and I hear machinery whirring. I wait. He returns and hands me the letter. I deliver it here. That's it. That's all I know. I don't get no extra pay or nuthin," whinged Tiny, shrugging his shoulders.

"Right, you can now continue with your errand. Act as you always do and then skedaddle back to the circus," Charlie told him giving him a little push around the corner.

Tiny trotted up to the gate and pulled on the rope hanging beside it and waited. Within a minute or so the grille opened and a hand in a grey glove attached to an arm in a grey sleeve appeared through the grille and gestured that it was ready to receive whatever Tiny had brought. Tiny withdrew the white letter from his pocket and jumping as high as he could deposited it into the waiting hand. The hand closed over the letter and withdrew through the grille. Tiny again took off heading back the way he had come.

Charlie had been watching these proceedings from the corner and waited till Tiny had departed before rounding the corner and scanning the fence for clues to what sort of a place this was. The only clue that Charlie could see was a plaque on the pillar next to the gate which read, 'The Distinguished Order of Cosmic Weavers'.

Charlie crossed the road and settled himself to wait and see who came and went. He didn't have long to wait. A few minutes later two figures dressed in grey from top to toe were walking down the street towards the gate of the Cosmic Weavers. They were female and their outfits consisted of a long grey dress, grey stockings and grey shoes. Around each waist was a dark grey girdle tied on the left side with a simple knot. Shoulders were wrapped in woven shawls of the same grey as the dresses, while a large scarf of dark grey was wrapped around the head and secured under the chin. No hair was showing. One was short and one was tall. On the back of each scarf was woven a large spider's web in the middle of which sat a large black spider with bright red markings on its back.

Charlie grimaced as he took in the details of what he was seeing. Charlie was a child of the bush and used to wildlife but this redback spider was also found in dark corners in city spaces and he knew its bite was venomous. He had to get back to Abigail and report what he had seen. He had no idea what Cosmic Weavers were, nor what they might be doing in there behind the wall with the contents of the letter that Tiny had just delivered to them, but he knew what he had witnessed today was important and needed to be relayed to the sisters.

A Safe Solution

Zarah had been waiting outside the Ringmaster's caravan till he left for his evening meal. When the place was quiet, she leapt lightly up the stairs to the door, took out her lock picking tools and skillfully picked the lock and opened the door. Once inside she wasted no time in making her way to the safe. She looked carefully at the dial with the numbers and drew her new toy from her pocket. This was the length of rubber pipe with a cone at each end secured with a small piece of string. She had read about these new safes with the dial locks and that what a safe cracker needed to do was to turn the dial to the set of numbers already set into the machine. Once the right number was reached a tumbler fell into place and the next number was selected. Zarah knew that the falling of the tumblers was not audible outside the safe, until that is, the safe cracker used a device to amplify the sound of the falling tumblers. Zarah had invented just such a device that very afternoon and she placed one end of it to her ear and used a piece of string to secure it there and placed the other open end to the door next to the dial. This left one hand free to rotate the dial.

Carefully and slowly she rotated the dial listening intently through her earpiece. There were ten numbers either side of '0' on the dial and it wasn't until she reached the number nine that she heard the sound she was waiting for. She expected there to be at least three numbers, so she kept up the process. Turning the dial to the left she listened intently until she heard the tumbler fall at the number five. Growing more confident, she turned the dial to the right again. She managed to just hear the number eight tumbler fall and she sat back on her heels. From outside she heard the voice of the Ringmaster talking to the small man they had met on their first morning at the circus. They were discussing the program for the next day. Hurriedly, Zarah removed the hearing device and turned the handle. The door swung open and she pulled a set of papers towards her. There it was, the bill of sale for the circus. She quickly opened it and read the names of the two people involved in the sale. Her eyebrows rose and she whistled softy through her teeth. Just as she heard the Ringmaster putting his key in his door lock she replaced the papers, shut the safe door and spun the dial a few times. She had read that this cancelled out the fact that an attempt had been made to break the code.

The Ringmaster and the small man entered the caravan and settled in for a long chat continuing to discuss business for the next day. As the Ringmaster farewelled his companion Zarah slipped under the bed.

The Ringmaster yawned and took a couple of strides toward his bedchamber, He pulled the curtain aside and sat down on his bed heavily. Under the bed Zarah made herself as small as she could and moved as close to the wall as possible. She just escaped being squashed and resigned herself to the fact that she had a long night ahead of her as she waited for the Ringmaster to sleep. Even then his bulk had forced the springs of the bed almost to the floor preventing her from leaving the underside of the bed undetected. She was there for the night! Or so she thought.

****

Zarah was slipping into a lovely dream about playing card games with her parents when she was awakened by a loud knocking on the Ringmaster's caravan door. She heard the Ringmaster moan before he rolled out of bed, shoved his feet into his slippers and shuffled to the door pulling on his dressing gown over his nightshirt and adjusting his nightcap. The Ringmaster opened the door and spoke to whoever was there. Zarah could not make out what was said as the conversationalists spoke very softly. The door closed and Zarah waited for the Ringmaster to return to his bed. However, all was quiet and she assumed that the Ringmaster had left with his visitor. She scuttled from under the bed and rushed to the window. Carefully she pulled the curtain aside to see the Ringmaster heading down Sideshow Alley towards a zeppelin parked beside the Big Top.

Zarah slipped quietly out of the caravan's door and sped off towards their own caravan. Did she have a story to tell!

Answers Raise Even More Questions

Beatrix had returned home from her visit with Mitchell very worried indeed. She arrived at about six o'clock in the evening to an empty caravan. Usually, by this time, all four adventurers were gathered together for the evening, discussing their activities for the day, exchanging information they had gathered and planning what they would do the next day. So, where were they?

Beatrix stood at the open door of the caravan and looked out trying to see if her sisters were coming. She sighed in relief when she saw Abigail hurrying towards her.

As she neared Beatrix, Abigail asked, "Beatrix, have you seen Zarah? She hasn't come home and it's starting to get late."

"No, I just arrived home myself."

Just then Charlie Buttons trotted up to the girls grinning. "Have I got some news for you," he said. Then glancing around asked, "Where is Zarah?"

"We don't know," answered Abigail. "We haven't seen her for hours and we are starting to worry."

"Let's spread out and check every place she might be, ask if anyone has seen her and be back in an hour in case she has returned in the meantime," suggested Beatrix.

The three went separate ways, asking anyone they saw if they had seen Zarah, but nobody had. They looked in all the likely places she might be, in the Big Top watching rehearsals or talking to the Chief Engineer. There was no performance that night so many of the artists liked to practice their routines or catch up with friends in the Big Top.

The searchers each returned to the caravan as it was getting dark and met up, all now very worried indeed.

"Well, let's share what we learned today and hope that she turns up," suggested Charlie, impatient to impart his newly acquired knowledge.

The sisters nodded, each unsure of what else they could do.

"Like you asked me to do, Abigail, I followed Tiny after he left the Great Gazaly's tent. He ran across the city and past the hospital. He stopped at a gate outside a large house next door. Just as he was about to knock I grabbed him and managed to get him to tell me what he was doing. He said he takes a note from the Ringmaster to the Great Gazaly who does something at the back of his tent and returns with a letter-locked document which he delivers to this house."

"What was in the letter? Do you know?" asked Abigail. At the same time, Beatrix wanted to know who lived in the house and what they did there.

"One at a time," said Charlie softly, "and not so loud. Do you want to be overheard?"

"Of course not. You're quite right. Please continue, Charlie," Abigail whispered.

"I am, as you may or may not know, a bit of an expert at opening and closing letter-locked documents. This one was just too easy," Charlie said blushing a little and examining his fingernails.

Abigail waved her hand, "All right, ramp up your pistons. Tell us what was in it."

"I can do better than that," Charlie stated and handed his copy of the document to Abigail. "I have no idea of what it is about, but you might, working as you do with the Great Gazaly."

Abigail took the paper and scanned its contents. "I'm not sure, but to me the numbers look like coordinates of some kind. I'll have to go to the Library to be sure. I'll do that tomorrow."

"And did you find out who lives there and what they do?" asked Beatrix.

"The plaque on the gate says 'The Distinguished Order of Cosmic Weavers', whoever they are," Charlie told them. "I waited to see if anyone came or went and I saw two ladies in grey wearing scarves with a redback spider in its web in the centre, enter through the door."

"Weavers, Cosmic Weavers at that", remarked Abigail. "What is all that about? Are they weaving those coordinates into some sort of cloth or fabric? And what for?"

Beatrix added, "And for whom? The Great Gazaly? The Ringmaster? Or is someone else giving the orders? Which brings me to what I learned today from Mitchell. He says we are in danger and should be very careful. He said he had sent us a note several days ago via Gregorio. But we didn't receive it. He didn't say so, but I got the idea that whoever has bought the circus is now running the show and is responsible for all the things that have happened to us, including kidnapping mother and father."

Just then soft footsteps could be heard ascending the stairs to the caravan and the door opened slowly, quietly and mysteriously. All three in the caravan looked at the door, drawing back in fear. When they saw who entered they fell upon her in relief. "Zarah," whispered Abigail. "Where have you been?"

"I'll tell you about it later, but first, you must hear this. I managed to open the safe in the Ringmaster's van and I found the sale deed for the circus and you will never guess who has bought it."

"Tell us please," Abigail pleaded.

Zarah looked around at three pairs of curious and plaintive eyes. "It was the Baron von Barbicon himself. We should have guessed it as he is the most prominent and wealthy man in the colony."

"Of course," murmured Beatrix, "we should have known it the moment we saw that flashy, super-expensive zeppelin moored outside the Big Top. We need our head gaskets checked. We should have realised it had to be him. "

Abigail frowned and spoke slowly, "Right then, we now know who kidnapped our parents because we recognised that zeppelin; and we know that the Baron is after us too.

We know that he is probably giving his instructions to the Ringmaster after which they go via the Great Gazaly to the Cosmic Weavers. What we don't know is what he is up to. What evil plan he has hatched, and why. This is what we must find out."

Leverage

That very same evening the Baron steered his zeppelin into its mooring position beside the Big Top. As this was the night off for the circus all was quiet and not many people were about. The days had been drawing in and it was almost dark.

When the Baron had purchased the circus, he had arranged a mooring tower to be built for his zeppelin. The Baron believed in efficiency, value and manoeuverability, and had patented his design for a modest-sized personal zeppelin some years ago. His design consisted of a rigid shape covered by a canvas envelope, an external propeller at the rear for propulsion, a series of separate compartments for passengers and cargo in the interior, a small steam engine and a series of small balloon-type containers containing helium which supplied the lift. As the craft was small the tower did not need to be very tall and stood only half as tall as the Big Top.

A window at the front tip of the zeppelin opened and a dark figure threw a lasso expertly over the tower's top mooring point. Other dark figures threw ropes from openings in the tail of the aircraft to the ground and shimmied down to tie the ropes to additional moorings secured in the ground. Thus, the zeppelin could be moored horizontally and close to the ground. One of the dark figures ran quickly into Sideshow Alley and returned a few minutes later. Both figures then stood to attention in preparation for the moment of disembarkation.

The zeppelin seemingly floated at its mooring, a black and malevolent-looking presence. The Baron's insignia glinted coldly in the silver moonlight. These insignia were fastened on either side of the ship and exemplified the Baron's sense of his own importance. Below the insignia could be just seen a collapsible portion of the front which opened to allow entry to objects larger than the relatively small form of its human passengers.

A staircase emerged from an opening in the belly of the craft and telescoped out and down to rest on the ground. The Baron stepped quickly down the staircase and stood looking towards the dark Sideshow Alley.

Shortly after a figure dressed in slippers, a gown and a nightcap shuffled up to the Baron. They held a short conversation and the Baron returned to the inside of his ship. The other figure shuffled back the way he had come.

****

Inside the ship was gloomy with only a couple of lanterns lit. As the Baron's eyes became more accustomed to the darkness inside, he made out two figures who were sitting together on a bench to the side of the zeppelin farthest from the exit. A man and a woman were tied together and to the bench, their mouths bound with kerchiefs.

"So, Dr Edgar and Dr Celeste, you have seen today in our tour over the circus that your daughters are alive and well and living in Melbourne. I have just spoken to the Ringmaster who has assured me that they can be retrieved at will and delivered to me, or otherwise disposed of, if that is my wish."

Edgar and Celeste struggled with their bonds, their eyes wide.

"I suggest then that you stop fighting me and do my bidding if you want to protect your lovely daughters. Are we agreed?"

The Della Morte parents nodded and slumped against each other.

What The Great Gazaly Knows

On her way to the Great Gazaly's tent the next afternoon, Abigail was thinking about what they had learned the previous evening about the Baron. What did they know about him? What was he up to? What was the Great Gazaly's role in the mysterious activities they had uncovered? Why did the Baron kidnap their parents and what did he want from them?

"Well," she said to herself. "First things first. The Great Gazaly must know more than he has told me. I'll tackle him first."

As usual, on arriving at the Great Gazaly's tent, she

cranked the handle and was admitted by the man himself and led into the back area where stood the Analytical Engine he used to calculate his predictions for the circus's customers. Abigail's job was to program the machine by preparing the punched cards needed to input data as required by the Great Gazaly. These cards were modelled on those used by weavers to produce the intricate patterns embedded into their fabric. In preparing the cards she was actually learning how to write programs to run the machine.

The Great Gazaly was standing next to the engine, polishing and cleaning the parts which was needed to keep the machine running at its best.

"Today," said the Great Gazaly looking at Abigail, "I want to talk about determining the probability of a rainy day tomorrow. How would you approach this question?"

Abigail frowned, finally suggesting that it could rain or not, so the probability would be 50%?

"Abigail, that is true if we know nothing about

weather patterns which might indicate the probability of rain. Think harder, how do we establish weather patterns?"

Abigail's eyes had lit up. She quickly replied, "Well, we could record daily temperatures, rain and other conditions and look for patterns there." Her mind racing, she continued, "We could, for example, look for seasonal patterns such as there might be more rainy days than non-rainy days in the winter. So ......, on any one day in the winter the probability of rain might be higher than non-rain."

The Great Gazaly placed his head on a side and said, "Excellent. I have been keeping records since I arrived in this country. I have the record I kept here. Please take it and look for patterns, then develop a program for the engine to forecast rain this coming Saturday. My favourite football team, Collingwood, is playing and they play better in the wet." He turned back to his polishing, smiling to himself.

"Oh, yes, I would like to do that. What other data have you been collecting?" Abigail shifted in her seat, "What about patents? Now that would be interesting. We could look at the success of patents for first timers or experienced inventors, or types of inventions that succeed, or ...." Abigail slowed down as she remembered that she had wanted to question the Great Gazaly on what he was doing with the requests that Tiny delivered and if he had connections with the Baron.

"Signor Babbagio," began Abigail, "I have heard rumors that the person who has bought the circus is the Baron von Barbicon. Have you heard them? Or do you know anything about it?"

The Great Gazaly froze. After a few seconds he recommenced his polishing of the cogs of the engine. He did not turn to look at her, but said "Where did you hear that? Nobody knows who bought the circus do they?"

Abigail was dissatisfied with this but decided not to press him and took another direction.

"I have noticed that Tiny visits in the afternoons; that you get busy; and then Tiny takes a message from you and runs off towards the hospital. May I ask what that is about?"

The Great Gazaly turned to look at her. "Abigail, there are dark forces at work in the world in which we live. I would suggest that it would be better for you if you did not ask too many questions about these happenings. I am not a supporter of the Baron von Barbicon, or his methods, but he has ways of ensuring that people do his bidding."

"Are you telling me that the Baron is forcing you somehow to do his bidding?" Abigail asked, suddenly concerned for the man she worked for.

The Great Gazaly dropped the cloth he had been using and clasped his hands together. His face lost its bland look and his eyes filled with tears. Suddenly he was sobbing as if his heart was breaking.

Alarmed at this, Abigail rose from her seat and stood up, moving closer to him offering her handkerchief. "Oh, Signore, whatever is the matter? What has upset you so?"

Signor Babbagio was weeping fit to blow a hundred

gaskets, his chest heaving and his body shaking. After several minutes of this he started to calm down. He wiped his eyes and blew his nose loudly, looking at the delicate handkerchief in his hand before stuffing it into his pocket. "So sorry. I will have this laundered for you," he managed to say.

Abigail leaned towards her employer and said in a firm and authoritative voice, "I think it is about time that we had an honest and serious talk about what is going on in this circus, don't you?"

"Yes, it would be a relief to tell someone, but the Baron must never know that I told you. He has a hold over me that he would not hesitate to use if it suited him. I fear him, Abigail, I fear him."

"I, also, have cause to fear him. I believe he kidnapped my parents and that his intentions towards them are not in anyone's interests other than his own," Abigail confided. Then looking directly into the man's eyes she said sternly, "I need answers to two questions. Firstly, what is it that you do for him after Tiny's visits? And secondly, what hold does he have over you?"

The signore breathed a huge sigh. "I don't know how I got into this predicament. I am a scientist, an inventor. I am an honest man, Abigail, really, I am. The Baron is not a good man. He is ruthless and cruel and will stop at nothing, I tell you, nothing," he finished, his voice starting to rise with emotion.

Abigail sighed also, "Signore just tell me what you know. I will not tell on you with the Baron."

The Great Gazaly nodded, sniffing loudly.

"Well?" Abigail asked expectantly. "Start at the beginning."

"It started the day that Miss Beatrix brought to me my new jacket. I received a visit from a young man with a slight limp wearing a bowler hat and mechanical eyepiece who told me that he was there on behalf of the Baron, the new owner of the circus. He was quietly spoken and very polite, but I was in no doubt that his words carried with them the weight of the Baron's determination. He told me that the Baron had work for me and that it was in my own interests to do what he wanted."

"What sort of work?" Abigail interrupted.

"It was just calculations. He said my engine would assist me. The calculations related to celestial bodies he said. When I enquired what the purpose might be of these calculations, he ignored me and asked to see my engine, my beautiful engine."

His eyes started to fill with tears and Abigail prompted him to continue.

"I took him through to the engine and he remarked softly that it would be a pity if anything were to happen to it. I took that as a threat! He was threatening my engine, my baby, my life. So, I agreed to do what the Baron wanted. He said that someone would bring me my instructions and I was to perform them immediately and give the answers to the messenger."

"So, what do you think these calculations are needed for?" Abigail inquired.

"I do not know. They are about where certain planets were or will be on particular dates. With the help of my engine these I can calculate using Isaac Newton's mathematical principles of the movement of the planets orbiting the sun. What do you think, Abigail?"

"I also do not know, but I will find out and discover where my parents fit into this plan of his, whatever it is. In the meantime, you must continue to cooperate and we may get some clues when we study his requests. At any rate, your secret is safe with me and mine," concluded Abigail.

Mitchell Digs

The Market Square was in full swing the next day. A marching band was making its way across the square to the sound of the steampipes which produced a noise similar to that of the older bagpipes but something much more raucous, although not unpleasant. As usual, shouts and screams were emanating from the Carousel of Shame. With the circus closed last night the thrill-seeking denizens of Melbourne had sought entertainment elsewhere and the Carousel had welcomed more than its usual number of occupants. The floppers had been very busy indeed.

It was not much quieter inside O'Connor's Patents Pending and Realisation Office where Mitchell had finished sorting the mail he had collected from the incoming mail chute located on the side door of the foyer. He was standing at the counter staring fixedly at a small letter in his hand. It was addressed to him and he immediately recognised the handwriting. It was from Abigail. He slipped the letter into his pocket and made his way through the workrooms to his own room at the back of the building.

As he had been accustomed to do recently, he blocked the door handle with a chair back and sat down to decipher his missive. He retrieved his Della Mortic Decoder from under his mattress, opened up the letter and began work. First he wrote down the code settings that came with the letter which read S,CCL9 and next he set his decoder to begin.

The letter read:

[decorative cipher text — four lines of invented script]

Mitchell frowned as he read this. What did he know about the Baron? Not much really. He knew where he could begin finding out about him though. He would start at the State Library and Patent Depository of Victoria.

One of Mitchell's responsibilities at his uncle's business was to deliver copies of approved patent designs. He knew there were three waiting to be taken to the Depository following approval from the Patent office. One was for a moving footpath; a second was for a clockwork personal fan; and the third was for a personal exercise machine which was in the form of stairs driven by the exercisers' providing the power source, their weight forcing the stairs down and around.

Every time that Mitchell went out from the business he knew that he was being followed by Trudie and

Rosalie. He also knew, however, that they would allow him to go to the Library as his business there was within the bounds of his uncle's orders. Once inside he would have a couple of hours to undertake some research on the Baron von Barbicon and try to learn how he came to the colony in the first place.

The State Library and Patent Depository was in Swanston Street which was just a few blocks from the Market Square. Sure enough, as Mitchell left on his errand he noticed his uncle's employees shadowing him. They didn't follow him into the Library but took up sentry duty one at the front on the steps leading to the main entrance and one around the back at the delivery bay. Mitchell tripped lightly up the steps and into the door marked Patent Depository. He had dressed for a late summer's day and wore his cream trousers and light tan jacket. He had dispensed with his usual vest for a pure white shirt open at the neck and with no collar. His boots were shiny and black and his hat was set at a jaunty angle, his blonde curls escaping beneath it. As usual he drew many admiring glances, but today he was oblivious to these as he felt his business was very serious and needed his full attention.

Having deposited his patents and completed the paperwork, he walked to the door. He had to navigate about ten feet across the entrance to the doors of the Library. Trudie was standing at the bottom of the stairs looking up at the doors. He waited for several minutes before her gaze turned away to a raucous argument going on at a stopped cable car. Mitchell quietly opened the door of the Patent Depository and moved gently towards the doors of the State Library. Before Trudie had turned back to watch the doors he had already slipped inside and she had not noticed his movement.

The Argus was a morning daily newspaper in Melbourne and had been since 1847. Mitchell reckoned that the Baron had to have been in Melbourne for at least fifteen years to have established the empire he now owned. He knew that the State Library kept back copies of the paper so he decided to start searching these backwards from 1873, fifteen years previously.

He found his way to the newspaper archives and charmed the newspaper librarian into assisting him to begin his search. The newspapers had been boxed by year; each box contained more than 360 daily newspapers. Mitchell drew down the box for the year 1873 and opened it. At the end of 2 hours he had scoured 98 copies and had found no mention of the Baron. He figured that at this rate of 50 newspapers per hour it would take him more than 100 hours to scour the whole fifteen years. This was too long, and Mitchell finally replaced the box. He had to find a way to narrow his search. He decided he needed to speak to his uncle and uncover what he knew about the Baron.

Uncle Patrick Remembers

Mitchell and Uncle Patrick liked to play a game of chess before Mitchell went to bed. Uncle Patrick sometimes went out after the game, but Mitchell never knew where he went.

That night the game was close with Uncle Patrick eventually winning with a cunning move with his knight. This put Uncle Patrick into a jovial mood. On the odd occasion when Mitchell had managed to win Uncle Patrick was very bad tempered indeed. Sensing his uncle's mood Mitchell asked casually, "I noticed that the Baron visited you the other day. What did he want if I may ask?"

"You may not ask, young Mitchell. The question of

the Baron is best left undiscussed," Uncle Patrick remarked, nodding his head.

"How long has he been in Melbourne, do you know? I ask only because he must have been here a long time to have built such a powerful empire. I have ambitions myself, you know," Mitchell nodded in time with his uncle.

"Well he is certainly a remarkable man, if a somewhat dangerous one. He must have been here ten years at least. No, eleven. I remember because the patent for his zeppelin was the first to be approved in 1877. I remember because there was something familiar about his design, but I couldn't place it. I must have been mistaken. It has certainly stood the test since then. The ship hasn't missed a beat, so to say. Anyway, I must nip out 'to see a man about a mechadog' before you ask. I'll see you tomorrow." And with that Uncle Patrick disappeared out the door.

"1877," murmured Mitchell. "That should narrow down my search. Back to the State Library tomorrow."

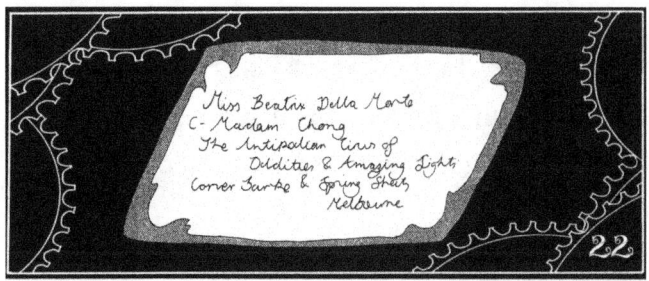

Miss Beatrix Della Morte
C- Madam Chong
The Antipodean Circus of
    Oddities & Amazing Lights
Corner Burke & Spring Streets
            Melbourne

22

Mitchell Makes Progress

Beatrix had received a coded message from Mitchell requesting she meet him inside the State Library and Patent Depository as he had uncovered something about the Baron which was important for them all to know.

She was excited about this for three reasons. Firstly, she was keen to find out what Mitchell had discovered about the Baron; secondly the fact that Mitchell had sent the message to her and not to Abigail gave her much pleasure; and thirdly, the prospect of seeing Mitchell again gave her a very warm feeling deep inside.

When Beatrix had told the others about the message and proposed meeting, Zarah and Abigail had exchanged a knowing glance and suppressed their small smiles. Beatrix noticed this and exclaimed, "What was that for? This is a serious meeting and Mitchell is just a friend, a friend to all of us, right?"

Abigail was quick to smooth over Beatrix's ruffled sensibilities. She said, "Of course, Bea. It's all right. I am worried about you walking the streets of Melbourne alone, however. I think I should go with you. What time is the meeting?"

"It's 10.30 am this morning," Beatrix murmured, "but I am sure I will be safe on my own. After all, it's broad daylight."

Abigail quickly replied, "Broad daylight or not, you are not going alone. And before you ask, Zarah, you must stay here. All three of us together make too much of an easy target."

It was not a long walk to the State Library: straight down Bourke Street, turn right onto Swanston Street to La Trobe Street. Abigail calculated it would take about 15 to 20 minutes.

Abigail checked the time with the spherical watch she wore suspended around her neck and said. "We should get ready and leave in 5 minutes."

So it was that 5 minutes later Abigail and Beatrix could be seen walking smartly along the wide streets of Melbourne on their mission, both nicely turned out, trying to merge with the crowds around them and oblivious to the tall dark figure which was shadowing them.

The Baron's Nephew

It had been yesterday afternoon when the Baron had greeted his nephew in his office. "My boy, it is good to see you. Your limp has gone, I notice. I knew when I sent you to Dr Prosthetico that he would fix you up."

"I must thank you, Uncle. It is indeed a relief to be pain free," said the Baron's nephew as he removed his bowler hat and eyepiece and took a seat. "It's also a relief to remove the eyepiece. You know that I had met the sisters prior to the Library of Wonder incident, and I have been using the eyepiece to disguise my real identity. They know me as Lieutenant Pasha Dimitrikov and do not know that I am related to you as well as to Aunt Blanche."

"No, I didn't know that," said the Baron looking closely at his nephew. "Anyway, tell me Jack, what of the sisters? What have they been up to?"

"I will, Uncle. But answer my question first. What do you want with the sisters? Surely three young girls cannot threaten your plans. I am not asking you to tell me what your plans are, but I don't understand why you are interested in the sisters," said the Baron's nephew.

"It is quite simple, nephew. Leverage, my boy. Leverage and insurance. I never commence a project without a backup plan," replied the Baron.

"Well, as you may know, they fled the scene of the Library of Wonder aboard the calliope trolley accompanied by Mitchell O'Connor, your friend Patrick O'Connor's nephew, and a young Indigenous boy. Somehow, they were able to join the circus and work with some of the performers," his nephew related to the Baron.

He continued, "For the past four months they have worked there quietly. Sometimes they go out, but not often. They have integrated well with the circus members and are well liked. That was until our visit to the circus where their standing in the circus community suffered a setback. Now, they hold meetings and snoop around asking questions. I am starting to feel somewhat uncomfortable in following them. They seem harmless to me."

The nephew paused and looked at his uncle, saying, "Are the rumours true? Did you kidnap their parents and have them hidden away somewhere doing secret work for you?"

"Nephew," exclaimed the Baron. "You wrong me. I don't have their parents and my only interest in the girls is to ensure they come to no harm. After all, I knew their grandparents forty years ago. Now what questions are they asking?"

"As far as I have heard they are trying to find out the name of the new owner of the circus," replied his nephew.

"Are they now?" murmured the Baron. "Well, please keep following them and report back to me."

Mitchell Delivers

Abigail and Beatrix arrived at the State Library and Patent Depository at precisely 10.30 am. They climbed the steps to the front doors and entered. They made their way into the great domed room of the State Library and sat down at one of the study tables. There were many people there before them. Reading newspapers seemed the most popular thing to be doing, although some visitors were deep into journals like The Melbourne Patent Magazine which gave monthly coverage of the latest and greatest patents to be approved in Victoria.

Mitchell had been waiting for their arrival and watched from the circular balcony until they sat down. He also watched as a tall, dark figure moved smoothly to a vacant table in the rear of the room. He then made his way down the back stairs and walked slowly towards their table evidently engrossed in a magazine he held before him.

As he went to pass their table Beatrix leaned over and whispered fiercely, "Mitchell, we're here!"

Mitchell dropped the magazine to his side and exclaimed quietly, "Miss Beatrix. Miss Abigail. What a delightful surprise. May I join you?"

Abigail nodded, "Of course, Mr O'Connor. Please do." And she waved to a seat opposite them at the same table.

Beatrix looked at him as he sat. "What's the matter with you? You pretend you didn't expect to see us this morning."

"You didn't come alone," Mitchell said. "You appear to have been followed."

Beatrix's head started swiveling, looking for their shadow. "Miss Beatrix, please. Don't do that. Please listen."

Mitchell now had the attention of both girls. "My uncle told me that the Baron arrived in Melbourne in 1877. This narrowed and focused my search. The Argus reported that in September of that year the Baron and Baroness von Barbicon arrived with no fanfare aboard the Voyager Ship Discovery at the Melbourne Town Hall terminus. The report indicated that they had left Europe under murky circumstances as instigated by a certain Dr Phillipe Dior of Paris."

"Dior?"exclaimed Abigail. "Grandfather! Our mother's father."

Beatrix was staring at Mitchell, her cheeks pink. "That means he not only knows the family but probably holds a grudge against us as well," she whispered. "He has probably been planning his revenge for years. Seeing that all our grandparents have already taken the last steam train, he is directing his anger at our parents and us. This is really shocking news."

"Shocking, yes, but also extremely illuminating," Abigail said softly.

"What we know now is that he has acquired two of the best inventors in the world and the means to force them to do his bidding, us. He also has the blueprints for a visualisation machine. He has access to a great Analytical and Probability Engine which is assisting him to weave some sort of fabric," Abigail listed these on her fingers. "You know what I think? I think that he is building something. Something that will benefit him and him alone!"

End Of Season

The members of the circus looked forward to the end of the Melbourne season. The summer had been long and hot, but now the days were cooling off and the nights starting to draw in. The circus was booked into a number of regional communities and would be on the road until they were due back in Melbourne next summer. Being on the road meant more physical work setting up and taking down the circus structures; on the other hand, it also meant fewer performances and more free time. The circus closed altogether over July and August before recommencing in September. A trial month had been scheduled in Ballarat for October under the leadership of the Ringmaster, however, with the change of ownership there was a widespread feeling of insecurity and fear among the members of the circus about what the future might hold for them.

Tonight's performance was therefore not as full of joy as in past seasons for the circus performers. Usually, there was an excited buzz around the caravans. Tonight, the buzz had diminished to more of a low and mournful hum. Where usually there were shrieks of laughter, tonight the air was filled with much shushing. Where there was usually to be heard the cheerful crackling of small fires, tonight the sounds of fires being extinguished and threads of smoke and fog wove their way through the night air.

Mitchell's uncle had relented and had given him permission to go to the final performance and Mitchell had called into the sisters' caravan to escort them to the Big Top. When he arrived, Beatrix was alone sitting on the steps leading up to the door. Abigail was already performing with the Great Gazaly. Zarah was at the Entourage Shed putting the final touches to the gleaming metal of the elephants and Charlie was doing last minute stretches for the Acrobatic troupe who appeared fairly early on in the program.

Beatrix had not seen Mitchell arrive. She had been thinking about her parents and was at that moment overcome with sadness, tears streaming down her cheeks.

"Miss Beatrix," he said. "Whatever is the matter?"

Beatrix quickly brushed away her tears and reached into her pocket for her handkerchief. She wiped her face and blew her nose, her colour now a becoming pink.

"Oh, Mitchell. I didn't see you there. It's nothing really. I am just being silly, missing my parents. I wish they were here with us."

Mitchell climbed the stairs and sat beside her. "I know just how you feel. I miss my parents, too. They are back in Ireland with my brothers and sisters. I don't think I will see them again." He put his arm around her shoulder, and she allowed herself to be comforted until they heard two mighty elephant trumpets announcing that the Great Parade was about to start which would mark the commencement of the final performance.

They had to walk around the entirety of Sideshow Alley to enter the Big Top. The atmosphere in the carnival grounds was heavy with smoke and swirling fog. The only light was provided by small lanterns suspended from the corners of the caravans casting shadows and dark corners. Beatrix shivered and the two moved closer together. Beatrix slipped her hand into Mitchell's and he squeezed it gently. The darkest areas were between the caravans. Two faces suddenly appeared out of the darkness. These belonged to the famous twins known as the Rodrigues Twins. The conjoined twins had been very successful on the European circuit and had been brought out to the colony at great expense by the Ringmaster. Normally they would smile at Beatrix and chat for a few minutes. Tonight, they faded back into the darkness, silent and unsmiling.

Members of the public keen to witness the Great Parade were jostling each other in their eagerness not to miss anything. In doing so they were ignoring the sideshows and pushing and shoving others out of their way. Beatrix found herself tripping and landing at the feet of the Tattooed Man. Mitchell helped her up and where once she had admired the tattoos of South Pacific scenes across the Tattooed Man's back, now she saw the scenes as wild and foreboding.

"I have a bad feeling about tonight," Beatrix whispered into Mitchell's ear. As she did so she noticed the World's Tallest Man staring at her over the heads of the crowd. His eyes followed hers, unblinking, till Beatrix and Mitchell had moved on.

The crowds were thinning as they neared the entrance to the Big Top and as usual the inmates of Sideshow Alley were following the crowds to enter the Big Top to watch the performance from the shadows under the seats. Beatrix looked behind her to see a tightly formed pack of sideshow performers trudging slowly and in step towards them. They all leaned slightly forward and low as if together they had taken on the form of a hungry predator stalking its prey.

As Beatrix and Mitchell burst into the light streaming from the Big Top, Mitchell turned to Beatrix, "I can see what you mean! Let's get inside before they catch up with us."

Final Performance

The Big Top was filled to capacity for the extravaganza that was the final performance of the season and the crowd was noisy and excited. Having finished with the Great Gazaly for the night Abigail joined Beatrix and Mitchell in the back row of the stalls.

As soon as Abigail was seated, Beatrix whispered to her, "Have you noticed anything strange tonight? Everyone's pistons and levers seem out of steamwhack. Even the Sideshowers are being weird."

"I know the Baron is here. His zeppelin is parked at

the aerotower," said Abigail, "and look, there he is with Mrs Crotchet-Smythe and Ursula her assistant and a tall young man in a bowler hat, who seems familiar to me, but I can't make out his face behind his eyepiece."

The brass band started proceedings with a short rendition of Let Us All Save the Queen. The young acrobats were circling the ring lighting the limelight spotlights set around the edge and the Ringmaster stepped into the ring. His uniform was blue with gold cording and tassels. His boots gleamed black to match his shining top hat. In his hand he held his golden trumpet. Lit from below his magnificent moustache sent eerie shadows across his face.

He waited for the band to finish and the crowd noise to subside then raised his trumpet to his mouth. "Ladies and gentlemen, boys and girls. Welcome to the final performance for this season of The Antipodean Circus of Oddities and Amazing Sights. We promise you sights you have never seen, sounds you have never heard and feats never before performed. You will be thrilled, terrified and shaken with mirth." The crowd applauded. The Ringmaster finished with "Let the circus begin!" With that the Ringmaster disappeared beyond the limelights into darkness.

Just then, there was a great commotion at the grand entrance. The magnificent steam elephants were striding in, their trunks raised and trumpeting.

"Look," said Mitchell pointing, "there's Zarah!" Zarah was indeed there, sitting astride the lead elephant in front of the driver. Madame Chong and Beatrix had just that day finished her costume and she looked resplendent in an Indian Maharani outfit in brilliant purple and yellow silks. She was waving regally at the crowd, with a double wave and smile to her sisters and Mitchell. The elephants were gleaming and presented the epitome of strength and elegance.

Just then Beatrix squealed and pulled her feet up under her. "Something grabbed my foot," she said almost hysterical. Mitchell tried to look under the seats and could just made out the band of Sideshowers who had followed them swaying and murmuring. It had been the World's Tallest Man who had reached up and touched Beatrix's foot. He looked up then at Mitchell and smiled a very toothless grin.

Beatrix was distracted and relaxed a bit when the band started up a marching tune and the Marching Girls were led into the tent by Suzette beautifully outfitted in orange and chocolate brown. She was twirling her sparkling silver baton and every ten steps the whole troupe stopped while she threw it spinning into the air and caught it neatly each and every time. The girls in the troupe were perfectly in step.

The young acrobats on the other hand were joyously throwing themselves and each other about, which contrasted deeply to the discipline of the marchers. The crowd loved them despite this and clapped and shouted gleefully.

There was a pause and the crowd quietened and looked expectantly towards the entrance. Then slowly the clownspringers entered led by Misery and stopped just inside the entrance. There were six of them and swaying gently in unison they scanned the audience silently. Finally, just as the audience was starting to murmur in confusion, Misery shouted and the clowns sprang into action. They literally sprang as they had steel springs attached to their boots. They spread in all directions, leaping and yelling. Most of the audience was laughing at their antics until the clowns started springing up into the aisles between the banks of seats. This signaled a change of tone in the performance and instantly became more threatening and a little sinister.

Misery himself stood still in the middle of the ring looking straight at Abigail, Beatrix and Mitchell. He then took one spring-assisted step to the edge of the ring and another to land on two springs beside the girls and Mitchell. He leaned his mournful clown face close to Abigail's and stared at her. Abigail recoiled slightly but held his stare with her own. He bent his head to his left and stared a minute longer then turned to face the ring and jumped down into it landing on two springs and joined the rest of the clowns in what looked like a competition of who could spring the highest.

By the time the elephants were exiting the Big Top the trapeze artists were entering followed up by

Professor Landers the Miraculous Memory Man, Brutus the Strongest Man in the World and The Great Bluey – Tight Rope Walker Extraordinaire.

The last to enter was the Ringmaster who jumped lightly into the centre of the ring to announce his first act. Suzette and her marching girls performed intricate marching routines and baton twirling and tossing with great precision and not one wrong step. And all the while the band played a rousing rendition of Click Go the Gears, Boys.

If the crowd was expecting the same ragged lack of discipline from the young acrobats as seen earlier, they were pleasantly surprised at the flexibility and sheer lack of fear the tumblers showed executing summersaults, cartwheels and group exercises. The acrobats were moving out after their performance as the Clownspringers moved in. Several of the acrobats hived off into the darkness under the seats and spread themselves around. These were Mr Flanagan's advanced group and their real work for the night was just beginning. While the audience was distracted by the Clownspringers the acrobats climbed onto another's shoulders to pick the pockets of their unsuspecting victims. So good had Mr Flanagan's tutelage been that wallets and purses were removed and replaced with the owners not even noticing that they had been robbed. Once the Clownspringers finished their antics with buckets of flowers and buttonhole water sprayers, tripping and leaping they dispersed around the ring between the banks of seats, some lounging in the aisles, others springing gently up and down, up and down as if ready to pounce on order

Next up was the Tight Rope Walker, The Great Bluey. He performed on stilts which he attached once he had climbed to the height of the tight rope. His balance was superb and his performance death defying. Finally, he fell into the net suspended under the rope and rolled over the edge of the net to receive his applause before stalking away into the night.

Mitchell sitting next to Beatrix had noticed the fact that the young acrobats and the Clownspringers were spread around the audience. He had also noticed some dark figures loitering in the shadowed areas between the seats. He leaned over to Abigail and Beatrix and whispered, "My gaskets are tingling.

Something sinister is afoot. I think that we need to skedaddle and fast." Before they could get moving, they heard an ominous sound; one they had heard before and recognised as the sound the jet packs of the floppers made when they were hovering, waiting to make an arrest. One landed in the aisle to their left and one to their right. There were Clownspringers in the aisles and under the seats were the Sideshowers and the Acrobats. They were trapped! They could do nothing but sit there and watch the rest of the performances until an opportunity presented itself for them to get away.

They didn't have long to wait. As soon as the Tight Rope Walker had made his way out of the tent, Misery sprang his way into the ring and stood looking at the tight rope and net. He summoned his fellow springers and indicated that they were to take down the net. Then he mimed to the crowd that he was going to walk across the rope himself with his springers on. The other clowns mimed that they were horrified and the audience joined in with "No, no, no!" But Misery ignored them all and started springing on the spot higher and higher until he was high enough to land on the platform at the end of the rope.

The crowd oohed and aahed for a while before falling silent. Misery stood on the platform making as if he was terrified. Gregorio, his second-in-command in clownspringing, managed to spring high enough to land on the platform beside him and tried to talk him down. However, with great show Misery stepped onto the wire and slid one spring out, then holding onto Gregorio slid the other spring onto the wire behind the first. Putting his hands in his pockets Misery slid slowly out onto the wire. He moved faster and then started to wobble, first one way then the other and back again. Trying to settle his wobbling, Misery spread his arms, then as if he knew his fate was inevitable covered his eyes with his hands. It seemed that what happened next took place in slow motion as he rolled to the side past the wire and ended hanging down from the wire from the bottom of his springs. Screams of horror had started up from the audience which then turned into laughs of relief and applause of appreciation which was thunderous. Misery had been hanging there with his hands over his eyes. He peeked through his fingers then theatrically spread his arms. Two other

Clownspringers were slowly releasing the wire so that Misery was able to slide down the wire till he reached the ground whereupon he sprang to his feet and performed his newly invented spring-chicken dance to the delight of the audience. He had just caused a great sensation and he could see the paths of glory stretching into the future.

Up in the back row there were three empty seats.

The audience found the thrill they had derived from Misery's performance lasted to the end of the performance and were very satisfied customers indeed as they followed the elephants, at the end of the performance, out of the Big Top.

Capture

The moon was full and bright outside the Big Top with some clouds swiftly moving across its face. A storm was expected. The Great Gazaly had sent around an announcement earlier in the day that high winds and some showers were expected around midnight. Hence, people were keen to be in their beds before it arrived.

Once the audience had dispersed and the performers had retired to their caravans, the sound every Melbournian dreaded could be heard in the descending silence – the swishing sound of jet packs. Moving in and out of the shadows, ten or twelve floppers were scouring the grounds, Sideshow Alley and around the caravans seeking the five runaways.

From their vantage point on the small hill with the jacaranda tree the five friends were lying close together flat on the ground and could see the terrifying sight of the floppers moving in and out of the shadows. They knew they were looking for them and the thought that they were being hunted was, in one way or another, of deep concern to each of the friends. Beatrix was overcome with sobbing; Mitchell was thinking hard of what their next move should be; Zarah and Charlie were very excited; and Abigail was filled with foreboding and despair. They dared not speak or move and every one of them was breathing hard from their desperate run from the Big Top.

The floppers were buzzing up and down, in and out, leaving no suspected hiding place un-searched. They also had an advantage in that they wore the latest in criminal detection equipment – goggles which allowed them to see in the dark. The goggles emitted a soft green glow which gave the helmeted heads of the floppers a sinister and threatening appearance.

Once the floppers had made a complete circuit of the grounds they gathered together in front of the entrance to the Big Top and formed a semi-circle of green-eyed monsters hovering and looking outwards towards vacant ground. Pulsating gently the swarm's gaze swept the landscape. The swarm was joined by a Sergeant with a huge mechadog on a lead. These beasts were programmed to follow the scent of humans and this one was straining on its lead This included the hill on which the jacaranda tree stood. The friends were holding their breaths and keeping as still as they could. Every few seconds a soft sob came from Beatrix who was covering her mouth to smother the evidence of her fear. Mitchell put his hand on her shoulder to calm her.

"I'll lead them off," he whispered. "You can all make a run for it once they are chasing me." He explained his plan to the others, stood up and started clambering up over the top of the hill.

With that the swarm was on the move. The floppers rose as one and made a V-shaped formation spearheaded straight to the jacaranda tree where there were now four on the ground.

Zarah jumped to her feet and shouted, "Run, run for your lives." She and Charlie took off in opposite directions. Two floppers peeled off from the back of the formation and veered towards them. Two more rounded the hill after Mitchell.

That left more than half a dozen, plus the mechadog and the Sergeant on foot, on course for Abigail and Beatrix. They stood together with their arms around each other, Abigail protecting Beatrix who was overcome with fear.

They didn't see the floppers surround them and hover in a small circle watching them, but they heard the swishing of the jet packs.

Abigail turned her head to face the six pairs of green eyes staring at them, silent, waiting for something. At that moment growling and barking the mechadog arrived pulling the constable behind. It was all he could do to keep the beast from jumping on the girls. Beatrix by this time was hysterical and screaming. Abigail was holding her and whispering into her ear that they would be alright.

The Sergeant nodded to the floppers and two of them picked up the two girls together and headed off back to the Big Top.

Meanwhile, Charlie had doubled back and was heading towards the Big Top. He heard the floppers close behind him and started to zigzag in an effort to elude them. However, the floppers were skilled at picking up escapees on the run so, easily, simply and in unison they scooped Charlie up and took off towards the Big Top.

Zarah had headed towards the Entourage shed. She heard the floppers behind her and dropped to the ground just as they were close enough to pick her up on the fly. They flew past her and she stood up. Knowing there was now no escape, she took the opportunity to face them to enquire about their see-in-the dark goggles. The floppers turned and hovered in front of her.

"I love your goggles! How do they work? Can I try them on?" she asked, but the floppers ignored her and smartly picked her up under the arms and carried her backwards towards the Big Top while she continued to ask questions.

Mitchell was used to being chased and picked up by the floppers. When he heard them behind him, he simply put his arms out and allowed himself to be captured and carried back to the Big Top.

Nobody managed to escape this time and all five were on their way back to face the Baron.

The Skipping Girl Beckons

Meanwhile, back in the Big Top, there remained four figures standing in the centre of the main ring. The great clean up would start tomorrow as the circus was due to move on to Geelong on Victoria's Corio Bay for a few days.

The Baron and his nephew stood talking to Mrs Blanche Crotchet-Smythe, the Superintendent of the Skipping Girl Home for Wayward and Homeless Girls situated in nearby Abbottsford and her assistant Ursula who was nattily attired in plain white shirt, white shorts and white sand shoes. Around Ursula's neck hung her whistle with which she used to communicate, particularly when on the run.

The Baron was finalising his instructions to Mrs Crotchet-Smythe, "…so if you could ensure that the girls can stay confined with you, I would appreciate it greatly. Their grandparents were great friends of mine and I feel a responsibility to look after the girls in their honour."

"Of course, Baron," said Mrs Crotchet-Smythe. "They will be safe with us and we will ensure they are kept busy and useful in our magnificent laundry," she simpered with as much of a smile she was able to produce. "Won't we, Ursula?" Ursula answered by a short blow on the sports whistle she wore around her neck.

The swishing sound of floppers could be heard approaching the tent. The first two flew in with a calm and garrulous Zarah in their arms. They set her down in front of the group but kept her arms contained in their steely grip. Zarah was not going to get away any time soon.

Abigail and Beatrix were flown in and set down. Beatrix was in shock and Abigail put her arm around her and comforted her.

"Well, found at last," said Mrs Crotchet-Smythe triumphantly. "We have missed you all terribly and are relieved to have you back with us once more. Aren't we, Ursula?" As usual, Ursula replied with a blow of the whistle.

Abigail had been staring at the Baron's nephew who had drawn his bowler hat low over his forehead. He had removed his eyepiece earlier to better see the performance and had forgotten to replace it. He did not really want Abigail to recognise him. Abigail leaned in to look at his face and could not stop herself saying, "You! What are you doing here with these people?"

Before the nephew could answer the Baron said ever so politely, "Ah Miss Abigail Della Morte, allow me to introduce my nephew, Lieutenant Pasha Dimitrikov of the Victorian Army. He was injured and has recently returned from the border wars."

Mrs Crotchet-Smythe interrupted, saying "He may be Pasha to you, but his mother, my sister, calls him Jack, as do I."

"Oh yes, we've met before," hissed Abigail. "Pasha, has your uncle told you that he abduc ………." Before she could finish her question, the Baron waved to the floppers saying that the girls needed to be delivered to the Skipping Girl Home for Wayward and Homeless Girls. When Mitchell and Charlie were carried in, the Baron stated that Mitchell was to be set down at his uncle's establishment where he was expected; and Charlie Buttons was to be returned to the Melbourne Boys' Asylum in South Melbourne.

Abigail resisted the floppers trying to grab her arms and continued talking to Pasha. "You knew that your uncle had scooped up our parents' boat into his horrible black zeppelin. You knew! No wonder you didn't come to see us when you returned from the war." The floppers were persisting but she continued to shrug them off. "Leave me alone," she cried. Suddenly, her rage spent, she allowed the floppers to pick her up but the tears in her eyes showed the depth of her despair at discovering that Pasha had betrayed her and her sisters.

Pasha raised his hands, "Abigail, you don't understand …." His shoulders slumped as he watched Abigail, her sisters and friends being escorted from the tent. Slowly, he turned to his uncle and lowered his eyes. With great deliberation he withdrew his eyepiece from his pocket and placed it on his eye.

The Baron had been watching his nephew. "I hope that you have not fallen for that girl. It would be most unfortunate if you had." Pasha placed his bowler hat on his head and said, looking straight at the Baron, "Of course not, Uncle."

Abigail looked sadly at her sisters. Yes, their parents were still missing and yes, they were being taken back to where they started, but they had learned a great deal in their time at the circus. She managed to smile when they looked back at her, "Don't worry, I've got an idea".

THE END

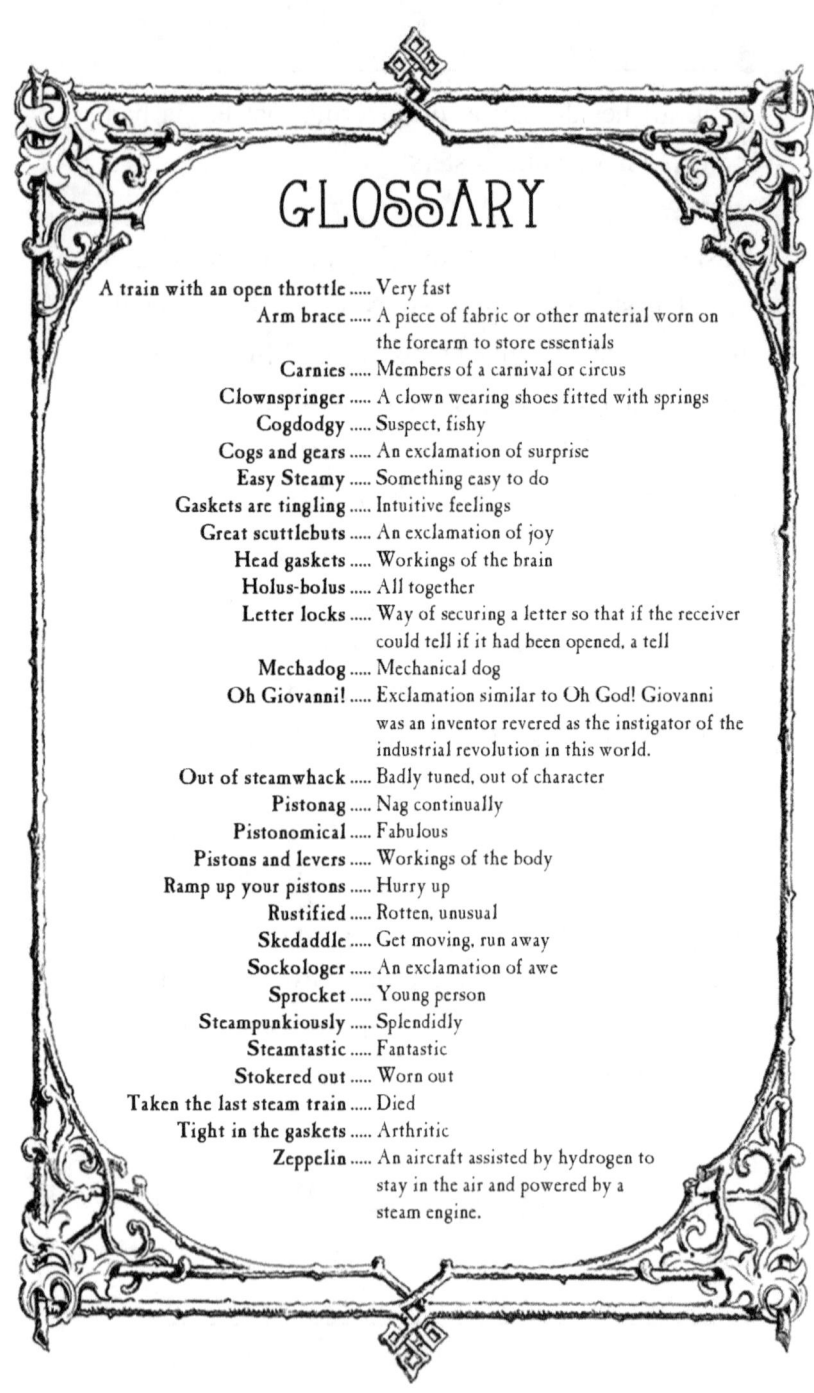

GLOSSARY

A train with an open throttle	Very fast
Arm brace	A piece of fabric or other material worn on the forearm to store essentials
Carnies	Members of a carnival or circus
Clownspringer	A clown wearing shoes fitted with springs
Cogdodgy	Suspect, fishy
Cogs and gears	An exclamation of surprise
Easy Steamy	Something easy to do
Gaskets are tingling	Intuitive feelings
Great scuttlebuts	An exclamation of joy
Head gaskets	Workings of the brain
Holus-bolus	All together
Letter locks	Way of securing a letter so that if the receiver could tell if it had been opened, a tell
Mechadog	Mechanical dog
Oh Giovanni!	Exclamation similar to Oh God! Giovanni was an inventor revered as the instigator of the industrial revolution in this world.
Out of steamwhack	Badly tuned, out of character
Pistonag	Nag continually
Pistonomical	Fabulous
Pistons and levers	Workings of the body
Ramp up your pistons	Hurry up
Rustified	Rotten, unusual
Skedaddle	Get moving, run away
Sockologer	An exclamation of awe
Sprocket	Young person
Steampunkiously	Splendidly
Steamtastic	Fantastic
Stokered out	Worn out
Taken the last steam train	Died
Tight in the gaskets	Arthritic
Zeppelin	An aircraft assisted by hydrogen to stay in the air and powered by a steam engine.

About the Author

GERALDINE F. MARTIN was born in Melbourne and has lived most of her adult life in the Canberra region where she raised three children, worked in the public service and designed hats and quilts. These days she writes stories, does papercraft and writes scripts with her three cats in her studio which is located right in the center of her garden in the country. She and daughter Marisa co-created the Della Morte Sisters and completed the animation Carousel of Shame in 2019, winning several awards including Best Australian Animation at Flickerfest Film Festival. This is Geraldine's third novel.

About the Illustrators

PAUL MARTIN is a trained artist from the Australian National University's Art School as well as a qualified electrician and an Associate Access Consultant. Paul prefers to use oil paints in his projects, but is also highly skilled in acrylics, multimedia and pen and ink. Paul is based in the Canberra region of Australia and has a lovely home studio from which he works.

MARISA MARTIN is a filmmaker, animator and illustrator based in Canberra, Australia. Marisa splits her production time between animation and live action projects. Her films have screened all over the world. In recent years, Marisa has focussed on animation, illustration, screen graphics and graphic design for film and television.

DELLA MORTIKA
CAROUSEL OF SHAME
The Animated Short Film

The Della Morte Sisters have been made into a short animated film! The 17 minute film is called 'Della Mortika: Carousel of Shame' and follows the sisters after they arrive in Australia and are sent to the Skipping Girl Home for Wayward and Homeless Girls (it is set between books 2 and 3). The Della Morte Sisters have their sisterly bond put to the test when jealousy rears its ugly head. The film is stop-motion style using paper puppets and pop-ups to bring the girls from the pages of the books into lively animation. It is available for viewing on our website: **www.dellamortika.com**

Steampunk Emporium

Della Mortika novels and other gearsome steampunk merchandise can be found at the Della Mortika Steampunk Emporium via our website.

WWW.DELLAMORTIKA.COM

www.ingramcontent.com/pod-product-compliance
Lightning Source LLC
Chambersburg PA
CBHW051130020726
47501CB00005B/1444